NARCISSUS IS DREAMING

A SCIENCE FICTION NOVEL

MICHAEL TAKEDA

PINK
NARCISSUS
PRESS

This book is a work of fiction. All the characters and events portrayed in this book are fictitious or are used fictiously, and any resemblance to real people or events is purely coincidental.

NARCISSUS IS DREAMING
© 2014 Michael Takeda

Cover design by Michael Takeda
Model: Jordan Tao Mambert

Published by Pink Narcissus Press
Massachusetts, USA
pinknarc.com

Library of Congress Control Number: 2014900023
ISBN: 978-1-939056-05-4
First trade paperback edition: May 2014

"She was a lipstick boy
She was a beautiful boy—"

> \- Born Slippy
> *Underworld*

"I've always said that a man who wears his
hair in a ponytail is a man who's not to be
trusted."

> \- John Ney Rieber
> *The Books of Magic, #8*

For Larissa Kinman
who asked the important question:
"What happens next?"

PART 1
DRAGON CELLO

The figure stands at the edge of the shadow, the comfortable darkness blurring the lines between background and body, shadows caressing the folds of its black clothing so that nearly no distinction can be made between animate and inanimate in the empty warehouse. It remains extremely still, its gray eyes unblinking – eyes as cold and hard as steel – as it surveys the damp street below, waiting. Only the eyes are in motion, flickering back and forth from one end of the street to the other, and one slim, pale hand which steadily brings a burning cigarette to its lips every thirty seconds or so, and then dips into the dark again, a cherry-red spark hissing like a warning signal against its thigh.

It twists its neck towards a sudden clatter from the street. It pinpoints the cause of the commotion: a rag-clad vagrant having knocked over a garbage can in search of second-hand treasure. It watches the vagrant in a clinical manner, without emotion, a scientific observer. The bum, seemingly dissatisfied with his findings, reels back down the street from whence he came and disappears in the night.

Now the figure is roused to action. It drops the cigarette to the floor and crushes it under its boot. It picks up the slim book resting on a chair to its right and brings it closer to the narrow crack of light coming in through the window, tilting it so the holograph on the screen springs to life above the tall, razor-sharp font of the title, blood-colored and wrapped in black barbed wire. It is not the title that interests the figure by the window, nor even the contents of the novel itself. It is only the holograph on the book's cover that captures the steel gray eye. The image consists of a young man strung up by the wrists with leather restraints, arms suspended loosely over his head. Knots of watery brown curls twist outward, creating a Medusa-like halo around his face, which is distorted in pain and ecstasy. His chest is bare, his frame tight and sinewy, and his mouth blurred, but it is still possible to see that he is attractive in a street-trash way, in a hungry-youth way. Inflicting this state upon him is a girl, equally young, hair dyed burgundy, lips taut with determination, brandishing a cat-o-nine tails. As the netbook shifts between its fingers, the whip lands on the bare chest of the boy and crackles back through the air again. The motion is choppy but the image is effective nonetheless. It stares at the holograph for a few minutes with that same clinical manner, then tosses the netbook back down on the chair. It reaches into the inner pocket of its tattered leather jacket and withdraws another cigarette.

If it could have been seen, which, of course, it had taken great precautions to prevent, anyone would have given the same description: a girl dressed in black with a long, blond ponytail coursing down her back, a little skinny, perhaps, and a face, although somewhat pretty, that had obviously never undergone a laser sculpt. A girl, age best guessed as mid-twenties, who probably couldn't afford a sculpt anyway, standing by the window while smoking a cigarette. If they could have watched this "girl" undetected for any substantial period of time, they might have noticed "her" unnatural stillness. More likely, they would have wondered what "she" was doing alone so late at night in the warehouse connected to Lion Productions, the largest film studio in Portland, Oregon, lurking in the darkness. But not even lurking. Not even blinking.

Not even human.

Eventually, finally, there is new movement, inside and out, when it spies a solitary man ambling down the deserted street. It slips farther back into the darkness, a movement controlled almost completely by instinct. As it watches the man walk down the street, almost below the window now, a twitch forms near its right eye, as though something were alive under the skin, a small bug perhaps, and there is something unnatural about that twitch – no, it's like the skin itself is alive, moving by its own volition. Even the figure by the window, so enraptured by the appearance of the loner on the street, does not seem to notice the twitch, does not reach a pale hand to touch its face, just stares at the man below. An indescribable intensity has replaced the clinical observation as it watches the young man who is passing below the window now; it can see only the top of his head, a head with watery brown curls twisting out snake-like in all directions.

It is the man on the cover of the book.

⚥

A calculating and hard edge gleams in the eyes of Max Pride, the man who owns and breathes the life into Lion Productions. Normally, many remarks are made about how Max Pride's soulful blue eyes overflow with warmth and kindness. But this is not a normal day. Max Pride has taken the director's chair.

"You call that acting?" he screams into his wireless amp. "*Baka* bitch, what fucking school gave you an actor's license? Obedience school?"

At this outburst, the temperamental lead actress begins to shriek and cry, cursing out a now indifferent Max Pride who lights a cigarette with an aristocratic flair from his perch in the director's chair. Having provoked no reaction, the beautiful, teary-eyed woman storms off the set, shoving best boys and gophers out of her warpath.

Max Pride checks his watch and shrugs to himself before scowling down at the drones around him. His amplified shout booms through the room. "Who do I have to blow to get a fucking cup of coffee around here?"

A heartbeat later, a girl with a baby-fine blond ponytail is holding up a coffee mug (with the company's logo: a lion reclining upon the words: LION PRODUCTIONS: *Work With Pride*) to the irate director. He clicks off his amp, unhooks it from his ear, and stares down at her. "You – what's your name?"

"Dahlia," she says.

"What department are you in?"

"FX."

He considers this most seriously. But before any further dialogue can be exchanged, the P.A. scuttles over and whispers up to Pride. "Max, baby. Something important's come up. You're needed in the conference room. Now."

Pride sighs. "Very well," he says, alighting from his throne. "Dahlia, bring my coffee."

The girl silently follows the director through the maze of Lion Productions, moving quickly, but careful not to disturb the steaming liquid inside the purple mug. They arrive at an unmarked door at the end of a long corridor and Pride shoves it open.

The room is small and empty except for a fading Cannes Film Festival poster from 2041 on the wall, and a long, metal table at which Kincaid O'Bryan, head writer and Max Pride's best friend, is pouring bourbon into a shot glass and fidgeting with an elastic band in his free hand, looking more glum and drunk than usual. Sitting beside him is a stranger with an olive complexion, a million-credit suit, and a black Mohawk. Towards the back of the room stands another well-dressed man sporting mirrored sunglasses, with dark, curly hair drawn back into a severe ponytail. Even though he is standing perfectly still with his hands folded before his crotch, he manages to emit an air of unquestionable authority. As Max Pride and Dahlia enter, the man with the Mohawk smiles widely, rising and extending a hand.

"John Nero," he says. "With Lights In Space. You must be Mr. Pride."

Pride eyes the offered hand but does not take it. He smiles gently. His smile and tone are not meant to offend.

"Mr. Nero, I'm a busy man. Get to the point, will you?"

"Lights In Space, Max," Kincaid says. "You know, off-world promoters."

"Off-world promoters," says Pride thoughtfully. He runs a hand over his shaved scalp. "All right, then, Mr. Nero," he says. "Sit down."

John Nero does not look like the type of man accustomed to taking orders, but he sits back down in his chair, still smiling. Pride takes the chair across from him. He makes a flippant gesture for Nero to speak.

"Since you are a busy man, Mr. Pride," Nero says coolly, "I'll skip over the usual preliminaries about how we admire your work, et cetera, et cetera, and cut to the chase. We might be interested in taking your new film off-world, if the material isn't too controversial."

"If the material isn't too controversial," Pride repeats slowly.

"They want to see the script, Max," Kincaid says through his glass, his voice thick, not from alcohol, but from fear.

Pride understands his friend's fear. Kincaid O'Bryan was always too sensitive for the spotlight, possessing a poet's soul and a mood disorder. On more than one occasion Kincaid had faced a sea of critics, crazed like rabid dogs for soft meat and hot blood, who had torn him into the unsalvageable shred of a man that he is now. Neurotic and unstable, yes, Pride knows, but, goddamn it, O'Bryan was a good writer, a fucking good writer, and he didn't deserve that. It had taken nearly two years for Pride to convince him to take up writing again, but only on the condition that no one but the actors and essential crew could read his rough drafts. "That's not possible," Pride tells them.

Nero tries to present his argument but is quickly cut off at every point. Politely cut off, which makes Nero falter. His ponderous brows begin to sink lower against his dark eyes. The smile has disappeared altogether. Pride expects Nero and his thug-like companion to walk away from the meeting at any moment – a meeting which is worth more money than Pride can even dream of – but then Nero says, "Maybe you can just tell us a little about the film."

"Shapers," says Max Pride. For a moment no one speaks and the word hangs in the air, heavy, as if on a tenterhook. Then Pride says, "Dahlia."

The girl blinks, then realizes that Pride is extending a hand for the coffee cup she is still holding. She passes it to him. He smiles.

"*Domo*, Dahlia." He runs his gaze over the all-black ensemble she wears and smirks to himself. "Black Dahlia."

Dahlia feels the gaze of the man in the back of the room as it falls upon her. She cannot see his eyes, masked by those reflective lenses, but she can feel them. She doesn't look at him. Instead she watches Kincaid twisting the elastic in his hand, stretching it over his fingers, compulsively knotting and unknotting it.

"Shapeshifters?" Nero asks, but he does not seem surprised. "But nobody knows much about Shapeshifters. Except that they've been outlawed."

"Exactly," says Pride. "On Earth, Shapers have reached near-mythical proportions, like Sirens or dragons. Hell, they were myths, only they were called something else, doppelgangers, metamorphs, a long time ago. Who knew they were real?"

"Maybe they aren't even real," Nero states.

"They're real," Kincaid says. "I've done my research."

"Maybe you're right," Nero says. "But I'm curious where you got your information. The factual information on which you're basing this film. Maybe you've been in contact with members of *AFAR?*"

Kincaid looks up from his glass, eyes watery. "A writer never reveals his sources."

"Ah," Nero says, and laughs. "Maybe some of your best friends are Shapers. Probably not. You probably wouldn't know a Shaper if it was staring you in the face, or so the saying goes. Tell us more."

"The Secret Service," Pride says, sipping his coffee.

"Excuse me?"

"Our Shaper works for the Secret Service," he explains, "as an assassin."

"An assassin?" Nero leans forward in his chair with interest. "You have quite an imagination, Mr. O'Bryan, I must say."

"It would be the perfect deception," Kincaid stammers.

"Perfect, yes," someone says with a voice that is all dark silk.

There is a gap in the conversation as some of them wonder about that voice. Everyone except Nero looks at the man in the back of the room.

"Forgive me for not introducing my companion," Nero says. "He's a man of so few words that I sometimes forget he's even in the room."

Dahlia finds that hard to believe. Even when completely silent, his presence is overwhelming, some sort of storm brewing below the calm facade, some mystery hidden behind the sunglasses. "Rush," he says by way of introduction (First name? Last? The newest designer drug which has been causing his quiet mood?) and takes Pride's hand, then Kincaid's, and finally Dahlia's.

She thinks that he has his hand clenched around hers for a moment too long, certainly longer than the others', as she studies his face. Beautiful lips which curl up into a feral smile, and a long, Romanesque nose upon which the unrevealing shades are firmly planted, are all she sees. Dahlia tries to peer past the mirrored lenses but sees only the reflection of her steel gray eyes staring back at her. His hand is as dry as cotton in the sun.

"Perhaps," Nero is saying diplomatically, "it would be possible for us to attend one of your dailies sometime?"

The elastic which Kincaid has been abusing suddenly shoots free of his fingers and flies across the room. Everyone pretends not to notice.

"I'll think about it," Pride says.

♂

Her name is Joyce Ann but she doesn't like it, a name that was not chosen *by* her, but chosen *for* her. Joyce Ann, from the time she was a child – not that she is much older than a child now – was always a victim of her own rebellious nature. It came as no surprise to anyone who knew her that, at the age of ten, she had said: *Fuck you, Mom*; and walked determinedly out the door, intending to never return. On the street, she renamed herself. She picked the name Asia, as it sounded totally foreign to her, totally unlike her old life.

So now, at sixteen, sharp as a razor, strong as bullet-proof glass, she needs no one. She is tough and lean and she knows she is attractive. It is more than the mirror that tells her so; it is the sultry, long looks from the men whose gazes pursue her. There is even one right now, lounging against the bar, watching her through the smoke and the pulsing lights of the ultra-hip club. She knows just what to do.

She sashays up to the bar, peering around for the bartender, just a few feet from her admirer. She lets her pretty mouth with its burgundy lipstick, a shade that matches her silky hair, fall into a pout. She leans up on tip-toe, raising the heels of her platform shoes off the floor, causing her little black skirt to hitch deviously up her per-fect, young thigh.

"Do you need something?" asks the admirer as he edges closer.

She turns to him. "Just a drink," she says, all inno-cence.

He moves closer still. He is hooked but not yet squirming. "Maybe I can buy you a drink. What's your poison?"

"I'd like," she says slowly, "a Wallbanger." She smiles. "A Harvey Wallbanger, I mean."

He returns the smile, revealing perfectly capped teeth. "I'm sure you'll have your Wallbanger."

Two Harvey Wallbangers later, there is one man knocked unconscious in an alley who has had his wallet stolen, and one sixteen-year-old girl who is intoxicated on alcohol and easy money. She scores some Euphoria and snorts it up in the piss-stinking bathroom stall. First it hits her in the front of her skull like a hammer before it spreads like fire through her veins. She tugs at her fishnet stockings and leans back against the wall of the dark club. The alternative techno-thrash beat vibrates in time with her pulse. She closes her eyes. It feels good.

When the song ends, she opens her eyes slowly, as if waking from a dream, and scans the club. When she sees the man who has just entered, she can hardly believe her eyes.

He is stunningly beautiful, young, draped in a shiny black motorcycle jacket, silky dark hair half-swept away from an exquisitely sculpted face, soft wisps of bangs accenting a perfect brow, angular cheekbones, and a chiseled jaw. Dark, liquid-like eyes that a girl could drown in, lips almost as burgundy as hers (Lipstick? Hard to say), torn-up black jeans, black t-shirt, and heavy combat boots unlaced in fashionable sloppiness. He hesitates in the doorway, eyes adjusting to the dark, glancing around casually.

All eyes follow him as he moves mercury-slick through the club. Asia is irked when he doesn't seem to notice her, his gaze skimming past her. He finds a place at the bar and takes out a cigarette. Almost immediately there is a girl beside him, a tall-haired Spandex creature of the night, offering him a light. Asia watches them, understanding the exchange without needing to hear the words. The Spandex creature says something that causes him to laugh, and laugh freely.

Kuso, *he's even more beautiful when he laughs*, thinks Asia.

Her pride can take no more, it demands satisfaction. Tossing back her hair, pursing her pretty lips, she moves to the bar as she has done before, leaning up on her toes, skirt hitching, keeping Mr. Sheer Fucking Perfection in the corner of her vision.

"You're right," he is saying with a voice like honey. "I'm not from around here."

"Well, then, where're you from?" asks the girl.

Seriously? thinks Asia. *Next you'll be asking him his sign.*

"Here and there," he says.

"How mysterious." She is nervously twisting the pendant around her neck, looking at Mr. Perfection in a most suggestive manner. "Are you a man with a dark past?"

"*Ie*," he says with his honey voice. "Everything is sugar plums and sunshine."

The girl giggles, but really she is far too old for a giggle to have any charm. Asia suppresses the urge to vomit and decides it's time to make her move. "*Sumi masen*," she says sweetly to him, "you haven't seen the bartender anywhere, have you?"

Now he looks at her. He smiles a heart-shattering smile. "Actually, I haven't."

"Have you been waiting long?"

He shrugs. "Not too long, but long enough." His eyes flicker over her but the smile is steady. "You know… I hate to say this, I really do, but it's true… your face is familiar. I do know you from somewhere, don't I?"

"Well," Asia says coyly, almost humbly. "Did you ever hear of a book called *Narcissus is Dreaming?*"

"Yeah," he says, then looks at her with a spark of recognition. "*Ne*, aren't you the girl on the cover?"

She smiles. "*Hai.*"

With mirth in his dark, thick-lashed eyes, he leans closer to her. "You look different without a whip."

Asia is pleased with herself. "Say, do you have another cigarette?"

The Spandex creature, having been forced to the sidelines, speaks up. "Aren't you too young to smoke?"

Asia shoots her a dangerous look. "Aren't you too

old for that dress?"

"*Busu,*" she hisses and attempts to grab Asia by the hair. But Asia is quick, despite the alcohol and Euphoria in her system, and twists away. She responds to the attack by slamming her fist into the mouth of the enemy, knocking her down hard and spitting blood. The Spandex creature howls like a wounded beast. A surge of power fills Asia as she lunges forward to finish the fight, but then the man is on his feet in front of her, her wrist caught in his hand. She looks at his face. He is smiling at her.

"*Kichigai,*" he murmurs. "Someone better get you out of here before you cause any more trouble."

There is a thrill like an electric shock where his hand touches the bare skin of her wrist. Maybe it is only due to the effects of the Euphoria, maybe not. Maybe it doesn't matter. "As long as you're someone," she says.

With a graceful hand he loosens his dark hair and lets it spill across the carpet like an underworld river, then reaches for the vodka bottle between them. "I've never had women fighting over me before," he admits.

Asia, relaxing on the beat-up sofa, looks down at her guest who is so openly spread across the floor. She doesn't believe him, but does not say so. "You can take off your jacket, you know, stay awhile."

He rolls his face toward her. "Can I?" he asks. He rises to his feet, unzipping his jacket and dropping it carelessly on the floor. He offers her a moody look. "Can I?"

"Oh, sure," she says. He is so perfect, she wonders if she is dreaming him.

He peels off his shirt, adding that to the heap on the floor. The silver ankh, dangling between his small, taut nipples, glimmers in the candlelight. "Can I?" he repeats, moving closer to her. He leans over the sofa, staring into her eyes which are full of awe, the ankh tripping over her breast. "Can I?" he whispers.

"Sure," she says.

He closes the gap, smears her lipstick with his own. When he draws back, she is breathless. He rubs his mouth with the back of his fist, leaving a burgundy smudge. "I need a cigarette," he says. He crouches down and searches through his jacket until he finds one, then lights it.

Asia sighs. "What's your name, anyway?"

"Dragon."

"Dragon what?"

"Dragon Cello."

"What kind of name is that?" she teases.

"A good one," he says, laughing as he glances over his shoulder. The image of him, crouching in the middle of the floor, glancing over his perfect, broad shoulder, is intensified by the smoke and filmy curtains dancing around him. He's perfect. A fantasy mod come to life. An angel. A god.

No, not perfect, she thinks, looking at his back. A strawberry-shaped birthmark, lumpen and dark, rises just above the skin at the small of his back. Asia has the sudden urge to touch it, so she edges closer to him, poking it with her fingernail. He jumps as if he's been burned, and whirls on her, much to her surprise, with ferocious anger.

"Don't you ever fucking do that again," he snarls.

♂

Max Pride watches the film as it rolls over the screen in the viewing room. Usually only he, his editor, and his best friend Kincaid O'Bryan attend the screenings, but not this afternoon. The editor also watches the film, her hand poised over the control box, ready to fast forward, rewind, and still frame at Pride's command. Kincaid O'Bryan, however, anxiously watches the Lights in Space men. Even in the dark, Mr. Rush retains his mirrored sunglasses.

There's something spooky about these goons, Kincaid decides. *What the hell do they want?*

"Money," Pride replied when Kincaid posed this

question two days ago, after the initial meeting.

On screen, the Shaper, played by a handsome, unknown actor whose name has already been forgotten by Nero, is creeping through an alley, wearing a long black trench coat and a matching fedora. He enters a hotel, all neon glow and ominous angles. Cut to a shot of a young woman in the elevator. Then a shot of the "Shaper" stepping out of the elevator alone. The "Shaper" walks down the hall, cranes his neck this way and that to confirm that the hall is deserted, and then he transforms.

The common term for what a Shaper does is not "transform," it is "shift." But what the "Shaper" on screen is doing is far too crude to be a shift. The transformation is rapid and violent, a marvel of a blend of CGI technology and cutting-edge prosthetic make-up. Nero can imagine the soundtrack that will eventually accompany this scene. A dark, moody kind of music, full of suspense. The Shaper's body shrinks, the fingers shorten and narrow as they sprout blood-red fingernails, the hair lengthens as it lightens, and the clothes melt from the trench coat into a long, blue dress by the same magical movie process. All at once there is great movement. Ultra dramatic and visually stunning, but, to anyone who has ever seen an actual shift, very unrealistic.

In the viewing room, at this moment, there is one person who knows what a Shaper's true shift looks like.

The Shaper on screen has become a woman. The audience easily recognizes that he has taken on the appearance of the woman from the elevator. She rings the doorbell and is admitted by two bodyguards. Dialogue. The film jumps.

"Sorry," murmurs the editor, not meaning it.

Pride makes no comment.

The Shaper is in the bedroom now, with a man. An important man, a senator of the United World Nation, according to the script. Not that Nero or Rush would know that, but that doesn't matter. What matters is the action. The Shaper moves to embrace the man and her hand transforms, becoming a series of silvery knives. She kills the senator quickly, her mouth against his to muffle his death gurgle.

A cut. The Shaper in his original male form, stooping over the body, drinking blood. It is shocking how erotic the Shaper's face looks as he lifts his head, emerging from the shadow into a spotlight, blood trickling from the corners of his mouth. He stands, rubbing his chin with the back of his hand, leaving a scarlet smear. He looks down at the corpse and then up as the camera zooms in on his face. A sly smile tugs at the corner of that wet, red mouth, as the skin near his right eye begins to twitch.

Mr. Rush speaks. "Would you back that up?"

The editor stops the film, backs it up, freezes the frame. "Here?"

"That's fine," Mr. Rush says. He leans forward in his chair. The vampiric scene is replayed. As the camera closes in on the actor's face, Mr. Rush lifts the shades from his eyes and props them on top of his head. He watches intently with his naked gaze. Kincaid is surprised how deep and sensitive those long-lashed brown eyes appear, with eyebrows gracefully sweeping over them as though painted on with an artist's delicate brush, having half-expected some deformity, either a birth defect or an eye-sculpt gone bad. Instead, Rush has the wide eyes of a doe, deceptively innocent, seeing everything.

But Mr. Rush, intent on the screen, does not see everything. He does not see an erotic expression on the actor's face. He does not see blood. He does not see a sly smile.

He sees a twitch.

He turns toward Pride, who is also startled by those unexpectedly beautiful and innocent eyes. "Could I talk to your special effects department?" Rush asks.

And Pride finds himself, despite his usual hush-hush policies, unthinkingly saying yes to Rush's request.

☿

It stands at the window of the warehouse, gazing down at the dark street below. Darker than usual because a gang of street rats had come by earlier and shattered four of the six street lamps with thrown rocks. Harmless fun to them. It had done nothing, felt nothing, while watching those vandalizing children put out the lights, although it had considered the inconvenience of the situation. Still, enough light remains on the street for it to see if the young man with the Medusa head will come. But it knows that he will come. It even knows when he will come. At 3:25, he will pass below the window, having taken the last Max train on his way home. He does this almost every night of the week, like clockwork. Every night of the week but one. There is one night he does not come home at all, a night in which the Shaper at the window sometimes sees someone else.

The girl with the burgundy hair, Asia. Sometimes she passes below the window, on her way to the same small apartment where she lives with the young man with the Medusa head. On those nights, the ones in which the young man doesn't come home at all, Asia passes by, sometimes alone, sometimes hanging on the arm of some other man. Two nights ago she had walked down this street with a tall, beautiful boy in black leather who calls himself Dragon Cello, both high on Euphoria and alcohol, stumbling and laughing.

Except that Dragon Cello had paused, albeit briefly, as they strolled down the street, to glance up at a dark window of Lion Production's warehouse, as if sensing someone's eyes upon them, but seeing nothing. Asia did not notice this distraction and they continued on their way, leaving the street deserted once more.

Now, waiting again, the Shaper thinks about its meeting earlier that afternoon with Mr. Rush. Rush had come sauntering into the FX department as if he owned the place. *Dahlia,* he had said with his dark silk voice, half-smiling, as if to prove that he remembered the name. Asking all kinds of questions. Asking the *Shaper*, not the FX department director, all kinds of questions. It did not trust Rush, but it feigned politeness. It showed him the work-room where they built the various prosthetics, then their hardware, the complex tangles of white boxes and black wires and exposed memory boards, and it explained how they programmed the "shifts" into the actor's real film image using the latest CGI technology. The tone of his voice expressed interest; the sunglasses hid all true intent.

Rush, decided the Shaper, was a real creep.

"And who dreams up this stuff?" Rush was asking.

"It's a collaborative effort," explained Dahlia, "we're all creative people."

"Of course," he said, nodding. He continued to ask questions that the Shaper answered smoothly, but the question about the twitch caused it to falter.

"A... twitch?"

"Yes, in the clip I just watched, at the end, there's this twitch on the guy's face. It looked like a mistake. I figured it must be a computer glitch or something. Didn't you work on it, Dahlia?"

"*Hai*, probably," said the Shaper. "But, really, I don't remember. We do a lot of work here. Many late nights. I'm surprised that I can remember *anything*."

Standing at the window, the Shaper replays the scene over and over in its head. It knows exactly what Rush had been talking about. What had unnerved it, however, was how Rush had latched onto such a minor detail and refused to let go, like a pissed-off pit bull.

It knows because it was the Shaper itself who had programmed the twitch. Mostly an unconscious decision, but now it seemed so careless. Had it really been on Earth, undetected for so long, that it was becoming sloppy? That is how Shapers are usually discovered, by letting down their guard and becoming all too comfortable in the human world. And Shapers have a terrible habit of choos-ing high-profile professions such as advertising, theater or film. Any profession based on the art of deception has a great appeal to Shapers, whose very existence out of the tribe demands deception, constraining them to take on – literally – a new form.

O'Bryan's depiction of Shapers was utter bullshit, full of incongruities and misconceptions, but of course it could not say so. Even when the "Shaper" was drinking human blood, Dahlia remained quiet. The truth is that Shapers are herbivores, and lack the requisite enzymes to easily digest meat. But it could not tell them the truth without raising suspicion.

But still – the twitch.

It had seen the twitch on the faces of its den parents at home in the tribe either when a shape had been held for too long, or under duress. Though it requires great con-centration to shift, the Shapers' ability to hold a shape is bred into its genetic code, and does not require constant conscious thought to maintain. Still, any stressful situation can result in a slip of the shape.

The Shapers are, by human standards, a queer race. Dahlia has learned that Earthmen tend to be suspicious of any race not divided into two separate genders like them-selves. Shapers are hermaphroditic, lacking any visible sex traits in their natural form. But the discrimination against Shapers is only partially due to lack of unidentifiable gen-der. Of concern to the majority of Earthmen is the ques-tion of Shaper morality, or, more accurately, the lack thereof. The original psychological tests had proven one thing beyond a doubt: Shapers are emotionally deficient.

In laymen's terms, Shapers have no feelings. And a creature who has no feelings about what is good and what is bad, has no sense of morality. A Shaper is indifferent not only to deeds of great kindness and beauty, but also to acts of unspeakable violence, which makes it extremely unpre-dictable and dangerous. Or so went the reasoning behind the law that banned Shapers from Earth and all United World Nation satellites and colonies.

But the real reason that Shapers are banned, some conspiracy theorists speculate, is because they cannot be identified, tracked or controlled by the government.

In their natural form, there is no way to distinguish one adult Shaper from another. They bear no distinguishing marks, no fingerprints, no distinct retinas. Their features and their skin tone, the creamy brown of milk chocolate, are the same. Every brain scan for every Shaper that has ever been scanned has turned out exactly the same. At first, the scientists who had come to the Shapers' home world believed the Shapers an inferior race. Their lack of verbal communication and the small size of their brains – brains the size of lemons – contributed to this assumption. Believing them inferior, the scientists permitted themselves the right to treat the aliens like animals, which led to the decision to dissect one of them, a Shaper child who had followed them like a docile cow to the slaughter. This resulted in a confrontation that ended in the deaths of the scientists.

The Shapers sensed, instinctively, that the young one was in pain. Although lacking the ability to feel emotions, they can suffer physical discomfort. So they remedied the situation in what seemed like the most efficient manner possible: threat to tribe – remove threat – no more threat to tribe.

Although some argued self-defense, the Shapers had not made a favorable first impression. In fact, the general populace of Earth, despite any fascination, had made their opinions on Shapers abundantly clear. Shady, shifting Shapers were not welcome in human settlements. Their only ally on Earth was the grassroots organization *AFAR* – Advocates For Alien Rights – headed by a charismatic and outspoken Earthman known as Calvin Pope.

Yet, despite Pope's efforts, Shapers were still outlawed on Earth. Those who chose to remain lived clandestinely, and permanently, in human shape.

This, however, is all ancient history to the Shaper in the warehouse. It has learned what it needs to know from the stories and eschewed the rest. It resides on the cutting edge of the present, waiting for the young man to pass below the window.

The Shaper knows the young man who passes, almost every night except one, below the warehouse window. It knows him well. His name is Thomas Echo and he used to be its lover while it was wearing the same shape – the Dahlia shape – it wears now. But Thomas Echo left it, never once assuming that the Shaper was anything other than human, for another woman: Asia, the girl who appeared on the cover of the book with him, a copy of which rests on the armchair to the Shaper's right.

The Shaper, as usual, is not looking at the netbook. It is looking at the street, waiting, as it has done every night for the past six weeks, for Thomas Echo to walk by. And he does. The same intensity alters the emotional deadness in the cold, gray eyes as the Shaper remembers certain moments shared with the young man: his laughter, his gentle touch, the manner in which he bit his lower lip and called out while tangled in the Shaper's naked limbs in the dark. It watches Thomas Echo walk down the street alone towards his house at 3:25 in the morning, something strange and dangerous stirring in the Shaper's alien soul, as the skin around its right eye starts to twitch.

The Shaper is impossibly, undeniably, unbelievably, and deeply in love with Thomas Echo.

♂
♀

Rush sits back in the booth, watching the head of his beer dissolve. This place, Club Whatever, had been John Nero's choice. Rush had accepted the invitation from the younger man with reservations. Sensing that Nero was a little uneasy with the Pride Project, Rush decided that by playing "big brother," he could attempt to strengthen Nero's resolve. Nothing annoys Rush more than a sign of weakness.

"I've just never been sent on a blatant spy case before," Nero was explaining.

"The security of the United World Nation is count-

ing on us," Rush says coolly. "Imagine if this Pride charac-
ter portrayed Shapers as some heroic, misunderstood
creatures, how would people react? Next they'll start taking *AFAR* seriously and demanding that Shapers be
allowed on Earth. Think about what would happen if that
motherfucker Calvin Pope got his way. Do you have any
idea how much chaos that would cause?"

"Man, you're right, Rush. It's just that when I joined
the service, I figured I'd be guarding the president or
something."

"You are, man," Rush says. "You are."

"Yeah," Nero agrees reluctantly, and reaches for his
beer.

Rush scans the club. *Everybody looks like they have
something to sell,* he thinks. *Well, they probably do.* He
notices a good-looking boy standing by the bar, chest and
arms sleekly sculpted from pumping iron on random
afternoons. Not a weak creature. Rush contemplates the
boy's admirable physical form for a moment before rising
from the table. "Gotta take a piss," he tells Nero.

He heads for the unisex bathroom and waits by the
stall. After a minute he pounds on the door. A girl calls out
hold your fucking horses and then she laughs. He waits
another minute before pounding on the door again.

The door falls open and a young, beautiful man –
without a doubt the most beautiful man that Rush has
ever seen – stumbles out. His dark eyes are full of water
and he's rubbing the side of his nose where, as Rush can
see, a trace of white powder delicately clings. From the
inside of the stall he hears the girl's voice again: "*Ne,
Dragon Cello, where're you going?*"

"Well, the Avon lady's calling," Dragon says. His eyes
slowly focus on the man before him. A furrow shoots
down his handsome brow as he stares at Rush.

"Have you got a problem, friend?" Rush asks.

Suddenly, Dragon's expression changes, the furrow
smoothing out into a mask of indifference. "No more than
anyone else," he drawls, teetering a little in his unlaced

boots. He balances himself with one hand against the doorway, turning away from Rush.

Asia appears. "Dragon, you forgot your leather," she says, handing it to him.

He smiles at her. "Well, you and that poison of yours make my head spin. I'm surprised that I can remember *anything*."

Rush watches them go, particularly the man. Rush is thinking. He is thinking about the strange way in which Dragon Cello looked at him, and about the last words the boy spoke. Yes, Mr. Rush is thinking that something good is going to happen to him tonight.

☿

In Asia's house, while she is behind the bathroom door, the beautiful, lithe Dragon Cello moves through the apartment with a purpose. He finds each clock and sets it back one hour. He assumes that she is too drunk to notice. Or at least he hopes that she is too drunk to notice. He's done everything he can to keep her from noticing what time it really is. The timing must be perfect. He stretches his body across the futon, closes his eyes, and waits patiently.

Unlike Dahlia, who was waiting impatiently earlier in the warehouse. But not waiting for Thomas Echo this time. Waiting, instead, for the crew to close up Lion Productions, for all the lights to shut down, and then wait some more. At midnight, the Shaper slinked silently through the empty hallways to the wardrobe department. It closed the door behind it and stood before the full-length mirror. It removed its clothes and folded them over a chair, contemplating its naked reflection. The Shaper let go of all thought and started to hum softly somewhere deep in its throat. Its body attuned itself to the hum. And then the Shaper shifted.

It was slow and gradual, piece by piece, taking over thirty minutes to complete since this shift was a more dif-

ficult process, involving a great change in height. It willed
its very bones, softer and spongier than human bones, to
elongate, and willed the flesh to accommodate them. Once
the dimensions were correct, it called for the excess flesh,
breasts and hips, to move inward and then outward to the
shoulders and biceps. Once the meticulous shaping was
finished, it willed the pigments to change – hair darkening, eyes darkening, full lips deepening – and sprouting
stray body hairs. Only the skin lightened, except for a
youthful rosy glow on the now prominent cheekbones.
The Shaper ceased to hum; its transformation complete. It
opened its now sultry, dark eyes and looked in the mirror.
It tested the vocal chords which had shrunk by will.
"Hello, Dragon Cello," said the Shaper to its perfect reflection and, then, smiling, entered the wardrobe to find the
black boots, the motorcycle jacket, and the rest of its
deception.

"Hello, Dragon Cello," Asia says now, having
emerged from the bathroom, climbing over it on the
futon, one foot on either side of its slim hips.

"Missed you," says the Shaper. "Thought I'd die of
loneliness without you."

"Sōka. Well, don't die yet." Asia laughs. "You have too
much going for you."

"Do I?" Dragon asks. It places a hand on either one
of her legs.

"Of course you do."

"And how do you know?"

"Don't be a drag," Asia says. "Can't you be happy?"

It looks at her deeply, with desire. The perfect photograph. The perfect lover. The perfect deception. "I'd be
happier, angel, if you were down here with me and not so
far away."

She smiles. "That can be arranged."

Later now. The clock says 2:20, and Asia believes it.
The Shaper knows better. It knows that the warehouse is
empty and that the last Max train has passed through the
stop. It knows that in five minutes, Thomas Echo will pass

under the warehouse window on his way home. But the Shaper does not hurry. It moves languidly, looking at the girl through its thick lashes, and slides a hand over her hip, throwing the sheets off the futon, revealing their naked-ness to the cool air of the room. The Shaper kisses her body, listening to the quickening of her heartbeat, almost instinctively knowing what she wants. The clock says 2:25.

The Shaper continues its movements against her, slides its body against hers. "Take me," it whispers. "Take me…"

She shudders, embraces the Shaper, lets it slide up inside her in its expertise manner. She writhes below. "I love you," it murmurs in the heat of the moment maybe, or maybe it doesn't matter to her.

"I love you!" she cries.

"And I love you, too," says Thomas Echo from the doorway of the room.

⚥

The Shaper flees.

It pumps those long Dragon legs, heart pounding, faster, faster, hair streaming out behind it, a blur of a man cutting through the alley, almost skidding at the corner, regaining its stride, and then keeps running. It isn't far to the warehouse, but the Shaper still runs. Its body is churn-ing with a thousand different sensations, none of which have to do with the slap of the pavement below those heavy boots, the whistling of the air turned cold against its face, or the heat rising with the exertion of its body. It reaches the shadowed side of the warehouse, climbs a garbage bin, scales the drainpipe, and grabs hold of the edge of the rusty fire escape. A fleeting thought passes through the Shaper's mind: *What if the window is no longer open?* But it manages to swing that long-limbed body out into the open air, to hook its feet onto the plat-form, and climb to the window which is still unlatched as the Shaper left it about three hours ago.

It slips in through the window and makes its way to the wardrobe department. Throwing the jacket on the floor, it crashes down in the chair in front of the vanity table, and releases a long lung-full of air as it stares at its reflection. Above its left cheekbone a bruise is forming, its hair is hanging in tangles around its face, and its eyes are wide and wild. It pushes the hair away from its brow which is hot from running. Shapers release heat instead of salt water from their pores, which sometimes poses a problem in hot climates. It knows that now is no time to shift, it lacks the will, the concentration, its mind scrambled. There is a sickening sensation in the Shaper's gut that it cannot identify, a heavy, lead feeling like it swallowed something too big to digest.

The unidentifiable feeling which torments the Shaper is guilt.

What do they say? the Shaper asks its reflection. Aloud it answers itself: "Revenge is sweet." *But why does it not feel sweet?* The Shaper feels physically ill when it recalls that look of hatred and despair on Thomas Echo's face as he stood in the doorway, while Asia scrambled into a robe, maybe not ashamed for what she'd done exactly, but at least ashamed for having been caught. But Thomas Echo was not really looking at Asia – he couldn't bring himself to do so – instead he was glaring at the intruder, at Dragon, who remained poetically sprawled across the bed in all his splendid naked male perfection.

"I would like… both of you… to get the fuck out of my house," Thomas said slowly, voice like gravel.

Only then did Dragon move, lazily, making a flippant gesture before he packed himself away in his torn-up black jeans, slipped on the boots and shirt, and picked up his jacket. In the background, Asia was crying softly, but Dragon didn't look at her, instead matching gazes with Thomas. It had never seen such anger in those blue eyes before, or the pain of betrayal. It stepped up to the young man, towering an ominous six inches above him, sliding into the jacket, and smiled smugly down at him. It couldn't resist delivering its last, fateful blow.

"Don't kid yourself that I'm the first," it said.

This remark cut deep, a critical wound. In response, Thomas struck out, slamming his fist against the Shaper's face, causing it to stumble back a step. It braced itself, ready to fight. "Come on," Thomas hissed, despite the fact that he was provoking someone much bigger and stronger than he was.

But the Shaper, despite the sting of its cheekbone, could not strike back. It realized in that moment that it could never hit Thomas Echo, whom it loved so desperately, in fact, it was sorry that it had even hurt him. In that moment, it understood what humans mean when they say that love is blind. The Shaper had been blinded by love and hadn't been able to foresee the ugliness it had created with this unpleasantly melodramatic scene. Confused by the consequences, it ran.

It wants to cry. But, although it had shaped the tear ducts that it has been carrying for the past eight years, they do not function involuntarily. It wills itself to cry. Two perfect tears roll down the beautiful face. However, the Shaper does not feel any better. It feels like a knife is twisting low in its chest, somewhere over its heart. It contemplates its reflection, wipes away the crocodile tears, and sighs again.

Then it sees a glimmer in the mirror that can only be someone moving in the back of the room.

The Shaper jolts to its feet as if electrified, ready to fight or flee. It sees the figure on the other side of the room, near the door that, the Shaper knows, is not the only door out of the room. There is another in the back, half-hidden behind the racks of clothing. It recognizes the man standing there, just as quickly as it recognizes the threat. The threat may or may not be the gun aimed in the Shaper's direction, held almost casually in the hand of Mr. Rush.

There is a moment of silent tension as Rush and the Shaper study each other, although the Shaper can only presume that Rush is watching it, due to his omnipresent sunglasses. Finally Rush speaks.

"I know what you're thinking. You're trying to figure out if those drugs you so carelessly took earlier will fuck up your chances of getting past me. You're also trying to figure out if you can take the bullet now and push it out later, granted that I don't hit any of your internal organs and kill you."

The Shaper is surprised. It was considering both of those things.

"However," Rush continues, "what you don't realize is that this is no ordinary gun. It doesn't fire bullets. It's what's known as a 'Disabler.' Do you know, Dragon, what a Disabler does?"

"*Hai*," the Shaper says, to keep Rush talking, distracted. "It's a hyped-up stun gun. Causes the nervous system to misfire, leaving the victim paralyzed for a few minutes."

"You're absolutely right," Rush says. "You probably also know that the Disabler model has been banned in several nations due to a few technical issues, such as how the beam can be easily modified to do more than paralyze the victim for a few minutes. With a five credit microchip, it could cause irreparable nerve damage. However, this particular Disabler has not been modified in that way."

The Shaper tilts its head. "Is that supposed to reassure me?"

"Not in the slightest," Rush says. His tone of voice remains very matter-of-fact, conversational, as though he were merely discussing the weather. "Because I figure you're smart enough to know that, in theory, a Disabler beam is an effective, even ideal weapon to use against the common criminal as it renders them powerless without causing injury or pain. But against certain other races with more complex nervous systems – highly sensitive nervous systems – the Disabler can cause a lot of pain. In fact, it has been proven to cause the most intense and gut-wrenching pain when used against Shapers."

The last word hangs in the air. The malicious, teeth-baring grin on Rush's face tells the Shaper that it has been discovered. Every nerve in the Shaper's body screams at it: DANGER! DANGER! DANGER! But the Shaper braces itself against its own nerves, forces an equally malicious smile, and says: "Fuck you, Rush," before it bolts for the back door.

Rush fires, misses, pursues. The Shaper runs, knocking down racks of clothes in its wake to obstruct Rush's pursuit. Rush leaps over the racks, does not stumble, and raises his gun to fire again. Dragon ducks the bright and silent beam. *Where is that goddamn door?* Heart throbbing, its nerves still shout their litany: DANGER! DANGER! DANGER! It gropes along the wall, finds the door, and jerks the handle.

The door is locked.

It can sense Rush almost on top of it, so, without thinking, following that blind instinct for survival, it slams its shoulder against the door with inhuman strength. There is a popping sound in the Shaper's shoulder which the Shaper doesn't even register, and the explosive crack of the door as the brass bolts splinter the wood, and then the door rips free of all three hinges and crashes to the floor. The Shaper clambers over the broken door and keeps running.

Sure-footed, Rush scrambles over the threshold and glimpses a blur of the Shaper careening around the corner. With an eye that leaves no detail unobserved, he notes the state of the door and, in the back of his mind, he admires the strength of the Shaper, the sheer nerve of the creature. Which makes the pursuit, and the impending capture, all the more attractive to Rush. *This is no ordinary Shaper,* Rush thinks as he gives chase.

The Shaper does not attempt to reach the warehouse window through which it has been coming and going. Chances are that Rush came in through the same window, since the rest of the movie studio is bolted up every night. Alarm or no alarm, the Shaper is heading for the front gate. It speeds through the hallways, cuts through Studio C, still furnished for the hotel scene. It jumps on the bed and then over, through the open doorway which leads to the studio hall, along the wall and out. Laser fire flashes on the doorway above its head and it stumbles. The Shaper falls, landing on the shoulder it had used to break the wardrobe department door, and pain shoots through it. It groans softly and staggers to its feet, stumbling through Studio A.

Studio A, the largest studio in the building, is encased in darkness. The Shaper can distinguish the familiar outlines of the set and the cameras scattered about the room, cables suspended in U-like loops from the lofty ceiling beams. Beyond that, the gate leading to the lot. To freedom. It can taste the freedom as if it were sugar on its lips. It grabs the chain to the gate – *Why isn't my left arm obeying the command to move?* – and, with one hand, jerks the chain. Not locked, but the alarm shrills as the gate lunges open, sailing up toward the ceiling, and the cold night air slaps the Shaper in the face.

It takes one step forward.

Suddenly Rush is on top of the Shaper. The Shaper hits the ground, the gravel on the lot cuts cruelly into its face, and it groans again as Rush kicks it in the torso. The spongy, soft ribs crack under the force of the blow, *snap, snap*. The Shaper makes an involuntary animal sound somewhere in its throat. All it can do is try to crawl away. Even though it looks pathetic, Rush admires its perseverance. He steps over the broken form of the Shaper, grinning as he lifts the gun and aims it at the Shaper's face. He waits for the whimpering Shaper to crack open an eye and look up into the mouth of Rush's long-barreled stun gun, into its destiny. The Shaper looks past the gun at Rush's face, seeing its own pain reflected perfectly in those twin silver lenses.

"You're not going to like this," Rush says and gleefully pulls the trigger.

Pain. Blinding, white-hot fire pain. The Shaper tries

to open its mouth to scream, let the pain out, gurgle a death cry, but its mouth is paralyzed, vocal chords frozen. It is convinced that it is dying. The pain is so intense and unrelenting that it wants to die, praying to whatever gods that are out there to let it die. It cannot move, cannot thrash, cannot scream. Inside, the Shaper is on fire, cannot breathe, cannot close its eyes to the pain; it is horrible. It wants to vomit from the pain but even its stomach muscles are frozen in time. *OhGodohGodohGodohGod ohGodletme die ohGod.* Everything wavers in the Shaper's vision, turning red. The Shaper, helpless, can only see the moon above its head, the moon turning the color of blood, and beyond it all, the alarm which is still screaming. It would beg Rush to kill it, if only it could.

Rush grins. "You've probably suffered enough," he says, close to the Shaper's ear, but his voice sounds distant, hollow, like he's talking from the inside of a tin can. He reaches into his pocket and withdraws a case. From the case he takes a syringe and plunges the needle into the Shaper's neck. The drug infiltrates the Shaper's system quickly, relieving its agony, and the Shaper is profoundly grateful as it slips from the pain into a warm, unsafe darkness.

PART 2
BLAKE

Light and pain. The Shaper opens its eyes and realizes that it is lying on a narrow bunk in a small cubicle
with bars on one side, much like a standard jail cell. There
is a small generator hum just beyond the bars which are
crisscrossed with a latticework of blue laser beams. It tries
to move, feeling the ache of its ribs and shoulder, and lets
out a moan.

"I'd be careful, if I were you," someone inside the cell
says.

The Shaper turns its head toward the voice. It sees a
girl, about nineteen years old, with long, soft brown hair
falling down around her shoulders, sitting in the corner of
the cell, her knees drawn up to her chin. She reminds the
Shaper of an angel in some painting it had seen in the Vat-
ican a long time ago. The Shaper opens its mouth to pose
a hundred different questions but instead vomits violently
on the floor by the bed.

"I warned you," says the girl.

Through the hair hanging limply in its face, it tries
to focus on the girl. Her wide-set blue eyes are fixated on
the Shaper, watching it clinically, unblinking, without
emotion. "Are you–" the Shaper begins but is overcome by
another fit of retching. Nothing but thick bile comes up,
sticking in its mouth, clogging and choking.

The girl with the angelic face stretches out her legs,
folding her hands in her lap, and waits for the sickness to
pass. "Yes, I am," she says.

The Shaper considers this while trying not to move.
"Do I know you?" it says.

A moment passes, and then the Shaper feels a tentative touch, questing and requesting, brush against the outer edges of its senses. A familiar touch.

"You were Damian?" she says.

The Shaper feels like crying again. "Yeah," it replies. "Hello, Blake."

"I used to be," says the other Shaper.

"Ah. Who are you now?"

"Blake is fine. And you?"

"Dragon. Dragon Cello."

Blake smiles a little. "I remember that."

"I always thought that would amuse you," Dragon says.

"I am amused, as much as anyone could be amused in this particular pit of hell."

"Where are we?"

Blake shrugs.

"What's happening to us?"

Blake shrugs again.

"How long have I been here?"

Blake tucks a strand of hair behind its ear. "About two days."

"How long have you been here?"

"They caught me about a week ago." Dragon does not react to this. It doesn't really want to know any more. Blake shakes its head. "Dragon Cello, huh. I think you just made my day. Not that it takes much in this place. What it lacks in decor, it also lacks in entertainment."

Dragon attempts to sit up, spasms of pain from its ribs nearly doubling it over. It manages to place its feet on the floor, but decides against standing.

"You look like shit," says Blake.

"And you're still a silver-tongued bastard."

Blake studies its new companion with a sharp, assessing eye. Perfectly proportioned, tall, solid. "It is a beautiful shape, however, even better than the Damian shape. My shapes never turn out that good. I don't know how you do it."

"This one took more work than the other one I was using."

Blake seems surprised. "You were swapping?"

"Was I–? Oh. I suppose I was."

"Really? How? You can't be honed already."

Dragon remembers Blake's use of that term. It referred to the most advanced level of skill shift, usually attributed to the ancients, Shapers of sixty years or more.

"No," Dragon says. "You know I had fifteen years when I left home."

"Dragon," Blake says slowly, "that means you're almost thirty: the age of conversion."

The implication that Dragon is almost at the age of conversion startles it. *Why haven't I thought of that before?* it thinks, but it already knows the answer. It had spent so much time with Thomas Echo that sometimes even the Shaper had believed itself human. "That's not good," the Shaper says.

Blake is thinking about this. "I'm glad I'm not you," it says.

♂

Rush sits at his desk, squinting moodily at the monitor. He mutes the audio before turning to the man standing across from his desk. "Lorenzo, what is a Dragon Cello, anyway?"

The Italian agent shrugs. "It's an outdated name for a spice."

"Lorenzo," Rush reminds him, "all Italian words are outdated now. We speak only English in the United World Nation."

Lorenzo takes the stab in his Italian pride and says nothing.

"Has the Shaper been given its options yet?" Rush asks. "How long has it been here? A week?"

"Yes, a week," Lorenzo replies steadily. "We were going to speak with it two days ago, but then there was the unexpected arrival of the other one – the Dragon one – so it seemed beneficial to wait. It seems that they know each other well. We hoped we'd be able to skim some pertinent information through the monitors this way."

"Have you learned anything yet?"

"They were very close. They have a sub-tribal bond, in fact. Except there's one thing that one of them said that's bothering the scientists. It said something about the age of conversion. Not a term we're truly familiar with," Lorenzo says, then adds, as an afterthought, "But you know how these Shapers are. They all come up with different words to describe Shaper functions."

Rush leans on his hand. "Was there anything else related to it?"

"I would have to check the transcripts."

"Do it," Rush orders. "What else?"

"The discs are ready to be implanted. All we need is your go-ahead, and, of course, the Shapers cooperation on the operation. Also, we have Agent Orange flying in tomorrow to oversee the Dragon project."

"Agent Orange?" Rush knows Orange and his reputation. A man who has turned many Shapers to the organization's cause. A man as devastating as his code name would suggest. If anyone could break a Shaper's will, it was Orange. Except…

Rush glances at the monitor, at Dragon Cello and Blake sitting on the bed in their cell. "Cancel Orange," Rush orders, much to Lorenzo's surprise. "I'll be handling the Dragon Project myself."

"Are you ready?" asks Blake.

Dragon nods and grits its teeth. Blake takes its dangling arm and shoves. There is a popping sound as the bone jumps back into its socket. Dragon groans. Blake lets go, grimacing as it rubs at the phantom pain in its own shoulder.

"Shit, that hurt. Did it work?"

Dragon lifts its arm, clenches the hand into a fist. It wasn't broken after all, just dislocated. The large purple bruises around its shoulder do not hurt half as much as the broken ribs. It would not be difficult to reabsorb the blood beneath the skin and make the bruises disappear, but they suited Dragon's mood as victim. "*Domo.*"

"Domo?"

"Oh. I was in the Pacific Northwest. Lots of Japanese influence. Curse words, mostly. *Sake* and *Sapporo.* That sort of thing." Dragon pauses, reaching up to scratch at its beardless jaw. "It just means 'thank you.'"

"In that case, you're welcome. It's not like I had any-thing better to do, anyway." Blake narrows its eyes. "Though it *did* hurt."

Silence.

"So, how did they catch you, Blake?" Dragon asks.

"It's totally stupid," Blake explains. "I was in Italy, acting in this theater production of *Six Characters in Search of an Author.* You know how I feel about Italy. I just had to go back, even though we're not supposed to stay anywhere for too long. But on opening night, I was driv-ing home from the theater in the director's Fiat and bam! I was hit by an ambulance. I wasn't hurt, but I was knocked unconscious. Of course the guys in the ambulance took me to the hospital and of course they took some x-rays. The next thing I knew, there was this strange asshole in a dark suit standing over me, telling me that I was a bad girl or something equally ludicrous. He flicked on the IV and I was out cold again before I could do anything, and I woke up here." Blake glances up at the bars as someone approaches; it is Lorenzo. "As a matter of fact, there's the asshole."

Lorenzo clasps his hands together, like a gesture of prayer. "You're breaking my heart, *bella,*" he says, his tone mocking. The Shapers stare at him, unblinking, humor-less. He stares back. "All right, down to business. You have a choice. You can either work with us or against us. And believe me, you don't want to work *against* us."

The two Shapers share a significant glance before returning their gazes to Lorenzo.

"What does that mean, exactly?" Blake asks.

He opens his hands. "You work with us, we train you, you learn a skill, and you even get paid a decent wage for doing important work."

Blake lets an expression of skepticism flash across its face. "Doing what, exactly?"

"Covert operations," says Lorenzo. "I'm not at liberty to say any more."

"And what happens if we say no?" Dragon asks. "You kill us?"

Lorenzo grins as though he's been waiting for that question. "No, we don't kill you. We do something far worse than kill you. We *cleanse* you."

⚥

Dragon slams its fist against the wall. "Damn you!" it roars. "Goddamn you all, you bastards!"

On the monitor in his office, Rush watches the Shaper pacing the confines of its cell. He notes how the Shaper comes close to the beams behind the bars – stun beams set at the same frequency as the Disabler ray – only to recoil from them instinctively. There is an expression on its face very similar to fear.

No, it is fear. It is a primal fear, thoughtless, like an animal's. No Shaper yet has ever willingly dared to suffer the effects of the Disabler beam more than once. Rush watches the Shaper sink down in the corner, trying to cover its ears to muffle the screams that penetrate the walls between the operating room and its cell. Rush is aware that this is a futile gesture. The Shaper may be able to block out the sound of Blake's terrible cries – always worse when they are in a woman shape, so high-pitched – but it cannot block out the sensation of Blake's pain.

They are sub-tribal, and the bond is strong. Not as

strong as if with a sibling or den parent of the tribe, but close enough to cause Dragon great suffering. Suffering because it senses its cousin's pain and can do nothing to alleviate it. If they had been strangers, had never touched, no bond would exist. But, fortunate or not, it does.

Fortunate for the researchers at the agency, at least. They'd never had a pair of bonded Shapers in confinement before, and were excited by the possibilities of new experiments.

Dragon suddenly jerks, scrambling to its feet, and spins around the cell. Its eye falls on a slim crack high up near the ceiling. It then pushes the bed, despite the lingering ache of its swollen ribcage, up against the wall. It stares into the crack, where the camera is cleverly hidden. "Rush," the Shaper hisses, looking genuinely enraged. "If you're listening, I've got to tell you something. I'm gonna make you sorry that you ever met me, Rush," it says, and, using the edge of the silver ankh it wears, smashes the lens of the camera.

☿

Then it is Dragon who is screaming, or at least Dragon thinks that it is screaming, but through the drug haze it is difficult to discern. The men throw its body down on a steel surgical table, bright lights flashing in its eyes, tongue thickened, *am I screaming?* It lashes out, they scuffle, movements slow like they are underwater, or caught in a dream.

Hold him down! someone shouts in underwater language and there is a firecracker blow to its jaw and underwater pain. First they took Blake then they came for Dragon. Dragon had tried to fight but they had grabbed it and drugged it anyway. *Blake? Where is Blake?* It calls for Blake, searching, searching. *Not fair, cannot sense Blake, Blake cannot help. Threat – no one to remove threat – help me...*

They slice through its shirt with a scalpel, prod its

body, men in green masks, they're the perverse scuba divers of this underwater world, one darksuit hanging on each flailing limb, another pressing its shoulders against the cold steel table, lights blinding, throat hoarse, dry, *my God I need a drink of water, my God you're going to kill me aren't you, let me go, letmego, Blake! Motherfather, Fathermother, Brothersister, Sisterbrother, help me! Not there*, someone says, *turn him over*, voices all distorted, radio static in the head, heavy-folly-spin-cloud-moon-blood-fly-shift head all full of water rushing into a grand ocean of space, and then they twist Dragon's body, *thud!* head hanging over the edge of the table like a wilted rose lilting on the stem, cold steel against its chest and another voice says: *Found it. Strap him.*

They strap its wrists and ankles to the table, corset-tight, then more fingers prod its back, the laser swings into place on its mechanical arm with a soft electric hum, and there's a call for disinfectant on a cotton swab. What happens next fills the Shaper with true terror. The disinfectant is applied to the area around that large, dark mark at the small of its back.

Earlier, before they came for Blake, Lorenzo had wheeled a monitor up to the bars and played a video for their viewing displeasure. It was a homemade film of dubious quality of what Lorenzo referred to as a cleansing. "What happens if you don't cooperate," Lorenzo explained. The video depicted a Shaper in a male human shape being strapped down on a surgical table, not quite drugged up to the eyeballs – no, this one was sober and fighting, trying to shift, the flesh rippling as if a hive of angry bees lay under the flesh of its chest. The laser hummed to life, firing down around the dark, strawberry-shaped mark that stood out on the skin below its ribcage, above the navel: its Shaper mark. Blake and Dragon had found themselves cringing; their own marks tingling as the laser cut flesh.

But the mark is not just flesh; it is a main component of the Shaper nervous system, a part of its brain.

There is no one central brain in the Shaper body that oversees everything. The lemon-sized organ in a Shaper's head controls only some of its vitals and its short-term memory. Other organs exist in the throat and torso, all intricately connected by a network of nerve fibers, but it is solely the organ on the surface of the flesh which allows them to shift.

The Shapers watched the screen as the shift organ was completely removed from the body and dropped unceremoniously into a steel pan to the side. An after-recovery shot was shown next. What remained of the Shaper was a hollow-eyed creature trapped in a sagging skin who had difficulty with its basic motor functions. Neither Shaper nor man. Empty. Nothing.

Lorenzo then tapped the top of the monitor with his fingers. "That one was one of the lucky ones. Retained most of its memory. We got it a job off-world in a miners' unit, digging up phosphates."

Dragon starts sobbing on the surgical table, a dry heaving that wracks its body. "Please," it begs. "Please."

Rush, watching the scene through a one-way mirror, has heard the word which has just fallen off the Shaper's lips. From experience, he can recognize when a Shaper's will is breaking, and what he's been anticipating. He clicks on the intercom and issues the order to wait.

Rush, gowned and masked, enters the operating room. He crouches down by Dragon's head at the end of the table. "Did you say something, Shaper?"

The Shaper sobs. "Please," it whispers.

"Please what?"

The Shaper pushes the words out past its thick, dry tongue. "Please don't cleanse me."

"You know," Rush says, "I thought you were stronger than that. Especially with that little drama you pulled with my camera. What did you say? Oh, yes, I remember." Rush's voice drops a cold octave. "You said you were going to make me sorry that I ever met you." Rush clasps the Shaper's limp head in his hands, tilting its neck to glare viciously down into its eyes. "You are mine," Rush says. "I own your damn shape-shifting ass. Do we understand each other?"

The Shaper tries to focus on Rush through its heavy-lidded eyes. "Yes," it says.

"Yes what?"

"We understand each other."

"Good," Rush says, and releases it. He heads to the door, snapping off the disposable gloves. After one more parting glance at the crumpled figure on the table, he nods at the team of surgeons. "Enough with the experiment. Put it under and insert the disc."

Dragon sits on the bed in the small cell, alone. An old-fashioned camera set upon a tripod just beyond the bars is its only company. Sometimes Dragon stares at the camera, a bulky black thing the size of the average paper-back book, with an eye the size of a quarter from pre-worldstate America, which tracks its movements through the cell. Mostly, the Shaper sits on the bed, not moving. Sometimes it eats, when food is brought to it by the ser-vice droid, and sometimes it sleeps for a few hours at a time, but mostly it sits. Eventually it loses track of time. Time has no meaning. Days pass. The Shaper waits. The Shaper thinks.

The Shaper thinks about Thomas Echo and Asia. The Shaper thinks about Blake. The Shaper thinks about its life. It thinks about its home planet and it thinks about the various personas it has created and the various lives it has lived on Earth.

It came to Earth eight years ago. Eight years ago, a perfect opportunity had been presented to the tribe. A human male by the name of Drake Yakamoto had ven-tured to the Shapers' land. Said he'd read what little was available about them, wanted to see what they were really like. He was not the first Earthman to ever reach the tribe, and many of the elders were able to speak his strange language. It was decided that Yakamoto could stay if there were a Shaper who could emulate his shape, and willing to take his place.

Yakamoto was twenty-six years old, working on a cruise ship as a waiter. The ship was docked at the City of the Cascades, several hundred kilometers away from any Shaper border. The Cascades was a Tiradian settlement, known for its great beauty, stunning waterfalls and natural rock crystal formations: a terrible tourist trap. The Tiradians were less frightening to humans than Shapers were, although rumors linked the bloodlines of the two races. The Shapers considered the Tiradians to be mutant Shapers, the Tiradians considered the Shapers to be mutant Tiradians, but each race kept to themselves, so all was well between these beings sharing a small planet.

The younger Shapers leapt upon Yakamoto with keen interest, touching his face, his heavy, black hair, his fingers, studying every centimeter of him intently with their pupil-less black eyes. He opened his mouth wide and laughed, causing the children to scatter. Who would take his place?

A fire was built in a field over which aromatic grasses were burned. The Shapers danced, emitting guttural cries and whoops, reminding the Earthman of an old movie from the twentieth century he'd once seen featuring Native Americans. He was entranced. He became steadily aware that there was a sound buzzing around him, a hum, also coming from the aliens. Then three Shapers stepped forward, each one indiscernible from the other with their smooth, brown hides, jutting jaws, and dull, unblinking black eyes, as though stepping out of the fire itself, and stood before him. Two other Shapers approached him from either side, gently lifting him to his feet. "What's going on?" he asked, but he was not scared, only curious. They stripped him of his clothing and then stepped away. The three Shapers before him then did something amazing. They shifted.

Bones elongated, hair grew – a living thing, an extension of the Shapers' flesh – skin lightened. He watched in disbelief as they became him.

Finally the shifting was complete. Abruptly the humming ceased. The three Shapers opened their eyes: three pairs of dark, slanting eyes were staring back at him. He moved closer to inspect them. The first one's face was too thin and there was something odd and unconvincing about its hair. The second one's limbs were angled awkwardly and the mouth too wide. Despite the other details being right, neither one of them seemed truly human. The third one, however, Yakamoto studied for a long time. The Shaper opened its mouth wide and laughed, as Yakamoto had done earlier, and then it spoke.

"What's going on?" the Shaper said. Its tone and inflections were perfect.

"Hello, Drake Yakamoto," the man said, and laughed.

This is what the Shaper is thinking about, how it became Drake Yakamoto – the only time it ever mimicked an already existent human being – when it has a living, breathing visitor for the first time since the operation. Lorenzo smiles at the Shaper as he switches off the laser grid and unlocks the cell door. "Rush wants to see you in his office," he says.

The Shaper lifts itself from the bed and follows Lorenzo through the building in silence. Lorenzo brings it to a door. "Go in."

The Shaper reluctantly enters the room.

The room is empty except for Rush's large, old-fashioned cherry wood desk, a leather sofa against the wall by the door, and Rush. The walls, wood paneled, are bare except for one impressively large monitor screwed into the wall. "Sit down," Rush says.

The Shaper sits in the offered chair, looking across the desk at Rush. Rush waits a moment before he reaches into his pocket. He throws a pack of cigarettes at the Shaper. The Shaper hesitantly reaches for the pack, eyeing

Rush suspiciously, then withdraws a Marlboro and sticks it between its lips. Rush leans over with a light and, as the Shaper ignites the cigarette, Rush seizes a handful of its hair and holds the Shaper still for a moment, staring through his shades at the Shaper's eyes. "How are you, Dragon?" Rush asks.

"I've been better," the Shaper tries to say, but its voice sounds rusty, dry, having been unused for so long.

Rush smiles (a sardonic half-smile that reminds Dragon of some painting it saw of the devil once in Germany) and releases the Shaper. "Everything has a price," Rush says cryptically. The Shaper does not dare ask him what that means, in fact, the Shaper decides that it would be best not to ask anything at all, and to just do what it is told.

"Tell me," Rush says. "Have you tried to shift?"

"No," says the raspy-voiced Shaper.

"Shift."

"Any particular shape?"

"No," Rush says. "No particular shape. Whatever is easiest."

The Shaper closes its eyes and searches for its inner concentration. It hums to focus and applies its will. But something is wrong. It wills its bones to change, minor bones, rebuild its facial structure, but nothing happens. Its eyes snap open, questioning Rush silently.

"I control that, too," Rush explains. "That disc we implanted, apart from being a tracking device, is also an anesthetic, the kind used in any long-term operation in a hospital, which is radio-controlled by me. Right now it is activated, for reasons that are probably clear to you."

"You don't trust me," the Shaper states.

"It's the nature of my training to not trust anyone. Which is part of the reason why we recruit so many Shapers for training. They have an obvious advantage when it comes to not trusting anyone."

"Training," the Shaper murmurs.

"Consider yourself lucky. What takes a man six years

of specialized study will be taught to you in six weeks."

The Shaper waits for Rush to say more about this training, but the buzz of the intercom interrupts the conversation. A man enters, probably one of the green masks, Dragon surmises, because, although he's wearing a suit at the moment, there's a stethoscope dangling from his neck. The men greet each other and then Rush tells the Shaper to get up on the desk.

The Shaper sits on the edge of the desk while the doctor peels back bandages, pokes and gawks, brandishing the cold stethoscope like a weapon – Dragon could swear that stethoscope had been kept on ice – and then straightens. "Those ribs appear to be healing nicely," he says. "Would you like to call up the x-rays?"

Rush taps a code into his console and a picture of the Shaper's insides appears on the large screen, a dozen shades of color separating one system from another. "Almost everything appears to be normal," the doctor announces.

"What do you mean by 'almost'?" Rush asks.

"In the eighth major nerve bundle," the doctor says, pointing to a knot-like clump of fibers located low in the Shaper's torso, glowing a pale orange-yellow on the screen, "there's a slight deformity in the size. It's a relatively recent growth, but it's not malignant."

Rush stares at the screen. "Then what is it?"

The doctor clears his throat, hating to have to admit that the new growth in the Shaper's main nervous system is something that they've never encountered before, and are uncertain of its origin or its function, although it seems to be harmless. The doctor declares that it might be dangerous to the Shaper's well-being to try to disentangle it from the eighth brain organ, so maybe they should just "keep an eye on it" for now, although it's probably just a fluke of nature, the byproduct of a genetic birth defect.

What they are looking at on the screen is more than just a fluke of nature. It is, although crudely formed, the Shaper's limbic system.

♂

To say that a Shaper has no limbic system would be an oversimplification. Simply defined, the limbic system is the principal emotional center in the brain. But simple definitions concerning the brain do not suffice because the brain is a complex structure which is still widely misunderstood. The same applies to the limbic system. This system is known to be extensive, including such parts as the thalamus, which relays information from the senses; the hypothalamus, which controls sexual urges and other motivational states; the hippocampus, which plays a role in learning and memory; and the amygdala, which regulates chemical and electrical changes in the brain that alters the way in which emotions are experienced and expressed.

Shaper neurology is even more widely misunderstood than humans'. Scientists know that Shapers do receive information from their senses, that they do succumb to sexual urges and other motivational states, and that they can learn and do have memories. So what functions the limbic system has in the human brain, are apparently contained in diverse structures in the Shapers' system. But the scientists also know that Shapers do not experience emotion, nor express it. So any presence of an amygdala is clearly lacking.

Except that there is a growth in Dragon's eighth major nerve bundle. The doctors do not recognize it as an amygdala because they do not expect it to be one. Therefore they do not question how a Shaper could spontaneously develop an amygdala and all the emotions that come with it. The fear, the joy, the sadness. The guilt, the regret, the love. Maybe if the Shaper were asked, it would say that this is the fault of Thomas Echo, with whom it fell in love. But did the falling in love cause the amygdala to grow, or did the amygdala cause it to fall in love?

♂

Two weeks into training, the Shaper is told that it will start its last class, "Disguise," on the following afternoon from 16:00 to 18:00. The Shaper shrugs. This class cannot be any stranger than any of the other classes that have been occupying its days.

Two weeks ago, it was sitting once again in Rush's office, being asked if it would like a more comfortable room. The Shaper was recalling what Rush had said about everything having its price, and was naturally hesitant toward any act of kindness. Rush went on to explain that Dragon would remain under surveillance as well as under lock and key – the disabling kind of lock and key – but it could make requests about its new environment, via a form to fill out. The form turned out to be an actual piece of paper and a pencil, since the Shaper was not allowed on the network nor access to anything resembling technology. Then Rush handed Dragon its schedule of classes and its eye cruised down the list. Dragon would have laughed, because it was so archaically high schoolish, if Rush had not been dead serious.

Etiquette:	08:00 – 0:900
Firearms and Weaponry:	09:00 – 11:00
Stealth:	11:00 – 12:00
Philosophy:	13:00 – 15:00
Toxic Warfare:	15:00 – 16:00

"Etiquette?" Dragon asked.

"I'll be teaching that one personally," Rush said. "As a matter of fact, it's time for your first lesson."

Rush took it to the showers. Although Shapers do not sweat, Dragon had managed to accumulate a fine layer of grime, some of it still remaining from the scuffle that had occurred with Rush in the parking lot of Lion Productions those many days ago – or was it weeks, now? Looking in the mirror, Dragon noticed that the welts from the gravel and all the bruises it had sustained on that fateful night had healed completely on their own. *Time, so much time, baby,* Dragon thought, a line from a book it had read and loved long ago.

Rush ordered it into the shower stall, telling it to throw out what remained of its clothes: torn jeans and boots. The spray was hot and delectable, and Dragon stood there a long time, as though it could melt and swirl down the drain along with the hot, soapy water. Rush called to it to hurry up, so Dragon shut off the water. There was no towel hanging nearby so it stepped out, water dripping off its lean body and creating small puddles as it walked naked over to Rush, waiting dutifully for another order.

Rush hesitated, looking at the Shaper in all its naked male perfection, body glistening clean and damp. It was a stunning shape, breathtaking. The Shaper sensed something in Rush's hesitation that prompted it to speak first. "Well?" the Shaper asked, and slid its hands slowly up its slim hips. Coyly.

Rush hardened. "Don't try to pull that shit with me," he said, throwing a towel at it. "Follow."

Dragon was then dressed in a white shirt below a black suit tailored perfectly. Next, Rush sat it down at the vanity table and they studied each other for a moment in the mirror, reminding Dragon of the times it had shifted at the vanity table in Pride's wardrobe department.

"Tie your hair back, but not sloppy this time," Rush said.

Dragon pulled its hair back into the slickest ponytail that it could, but the soft feminine wisps refused to be tied.

"You're too beautiful," Rush said in such a way that it was not a compliment. "Too conspicuous. There's no way you would *not* stand out in a crowd. You'll need a new shape eventually, but for now I guess I'll have to make do with this."

So began Dragon's education. Most of its classes were one on one, except for philosophy, which was taken with Blake. Unable to sense Blake since their separation, Dragon was relieved to discover that Blake had not been cleansed either. Every day for two hours, the Shapers would sit next to each other, neither looking at each other nor talking, but able, in such close proximity, to feel each other's familiar presence with their Shaper senses.

The coursework itself was not philosophy in any real sense; it was a history class punctuated with lessons on how agents were supposed to think. How the Shapers were supposed to think from now on. Mild brainwashing. Early on, they learned that they were not involved directly with the Secret Service. In fact, the organization overseeing their training was even more covert, so the Secret Service was largely unaware of its existence, as were most of the other government agencies.

Eventually Blake and Dragon were given permission to visit each other in the evenings, an hour or two usually spent in Dragon's room.

The room, not much larger than the holding cell, but large enough to be an improvement, was a bit stark. It contained a bed, a desk, a chair, and a small halogen lamp, although it contained a separate bathroom with an actual bathtub and, best of all, no camera hidden among the pristine white tile. Since moving in, Dragon had indeed filled out the request forms, and now there were personal touches to the room, including a few of its favorite books, such as *The Left Hand of Darkness* by Ursula K. LeGuin, *Imajica* by Clive Barker, *The Dancers at the End of Time* by Michael Moorcock, *Venus Plus X* by William Sturgeon, several books by Robert Silverberg and Storm Constantine, as well as some pop-psychology books including the once highly popular *Women are from Venus, Men are from Mars*. Rush had flipped through them before handing them over, not really surprised that the novels described creatures that either switched shape or switched genders. Most of the books the Shaper requested were impossible to find. Printing had gone out of fashion several decades ago, so paper copies had become collector's items. Fortunately, the agency's overhead was low and its budget large, so it made no damn difference to Rush if the Shaper had a costly reading habit, or if it demanded a bathtub full of diamonds and a stack of rare esoteric porn.

Other than the books, Dragon had requested a sketchbook and some pencils, a few cartons of cigarettes, and "something for the walls," which turned out to be a reproduction of Salvador Dali's *The Metamorphosis of Narcissus*, and an old poster of a musician from the twentieth century called David Bowie.

Dragon would sometimes pass the evening sketching Blake, or they would talk about the past, reminiscing about their travels through Europe during their nine months together. They would often lie on Dragon's bed, curled up, Blake's back to Dragon's chest, Blake recounting stories from the books it had read. Blake had a penchant for romance novels. All that love and emotion was a mystery to it, and the jealousy, that was just amazing.

On the day that Dragon finds out that it will begin attending the Disguise class (whatever that is), this is how it passes the evening, curled up like a lover against Blake's back, half-listening to Blake talk about the new twists in the emotional landscapes of the characters in the romance novel it is currently reading.

"There's one thing I don't understand," Blake says. "If love is supposed to be this wonderful emotion that everybody wants, why is everybody made so miserable by it?"

Dragon sighs against Blake's neck. "They say that love and hate go together. Where there is one, there is often the other."

"Do they say that?"

"Somebody must have said it once."

"Somebody must have said everything at least once," Blake says. "And what's with this whole human issue of tying reproduction to love, anyway? It's been proven that better children can be created in laboratories, but hardly anyone wants to do it that way. Most humans prefer copulation."

"It's complicated. It has to do with religion as well as love," Dragon says. "Forget about it. They're just different from us."

Blake sits up, eyeballing Dragon with curious intent. "Did you ever enjoy it?"

"Enjoy what?"

"What have I just been talking about?"

"You mean fucking."

Blake rolls its eyes. "Stop being so difficult. Of course that's what I mean."

Dragon thinks about it. It thinks about Thomas Echo and its lovers before him, both male and female. "I guess so," it says. "As a part of the deception, in an aesthetic sense. It interests me to see how their behavior changes during sex, like they are another person altogether. I wonder what the pleasure feels like, orgasm and all that. I've always wanted to experience one. Haven't you?"

Blake considers the mystery of sexual pleasure. "They have drugs that simulate that. Ever hear of Hammer?"

"No."

"I heard it's like that, a big hammer of an orgasm, like Euphoria or Ecstasy, but all at once."

"Would it work that way on us?"

"Don't know," Blake says. "But I don't want to be the first Shaper to try it. Remember what happened to the first one of us to try LSD? DOA."

Dragon reaches out and pulls Blake back down to the bed, whispering in its ear. "I think Rush wants me."

Blake rolls over, staring with its cold angelic eyes, considering the possible advantages and disadvantages of the situation, then nestles its head on the broad shoulder, whispering back to Dragon.

"Go for it," Blake says.

⚦

It is during Disguise class that Dragon encounters another Shaper.

The Shaper, wearing the guise of a sharp-boned, red-haired woman, striking but not attractive, with eyes so pale that they seem like the sun had bleached most of the color out of them, is not formally introduced to Dragon. Names are not important here. This Shaper has already graduated from the program, and is only present for the demonstration.

"Watch closely," Rush says. "You're only going to see this once."

"I'm watching."

"Are you ready?" asks Rush, this directed to the other Shaper.

"Ready," it replies, and then, suddenly, it shifts.

Suddenly is not an understatement. Without a warning, without a hum or even a blink, the Shaper standing before Dragon shifts, and it is a shift like no other it has ever seen, or even heard of, except maybe in Max Pride's movie, *but, damn, I thought that we were making it up.* It is a crass, violent transformation, devoid of any beauty. It is terrifying. Dragon feels weak to its stomach just watching it, *it's all so… unnatural.* The shift itself does not take the requisite thirty minutes. It takes three.

The shape, Dragon notices, is shaky. It was too fast, impossibly fast.

"We have developed a drug," Rush explains, "that can speed up a shift. We will teach you how to use it. You will need it."

No, Dragon is thinking, *no, I don't want to do that, it's not normal, it's not right.* But it will not argue with Rush. Not now.

Everything has a price, Dragon thinks.

Dragon passes another week, adeptly going through

the motions of its enforced routine, while it formulates a plan to avoid being subjected to the speed drug. It decides that there is only one channel through which it can go, and that channel is Rush.

At the end of Disguise class, when Dragon is supposed to return to its room, it lingers in the doorway, hands in pockets, staring at the floor.

"What is it?" Rush finally asks.

Dragon does not look up. "I have a request."

"You know the procedure," Rush says. "Fill out the form and bring it to me in the morning."

"Oh, come on, Rush," the Shaper whines.

"Excuse me?"

"I'm tired of filling out forms. Besides, it's just one little thing." Now Dragon looks up at Rush expectantly, but not too expectantly. "Look, I'm just in the mood for a glass of wine tonight, and with all this paperwork I have to fill out, by the time I get the wine, it's going to be next Thursday."

Rush does not respond.

"Am I asking for too much? Haven't I done enough to deserve a glass of wine?"

"Suppose you have," Rush says slowly. "Where am I supposed to procure this wine?"

"Supermarket?" Dragon suggests.

"There isn't one close by."

"Liquor store?"

Rush shakes his head.

"Lorenzo's room?"

Rush grins with his usual cold devil charm. "I've got a meeting to attend. Get back to your room before I kick your ass."

♂

Four hours later there is a knock on the door. Dragon leans over to set its sketchbook on the desk and gets up to answer. Rush, having shut off the stun beams, stands in the stark corridor with a bottle of wine in one hand and two wine glasses in the other. "Room fucking service," he says lightly, handing everything over.

"Didn't expect to see *you*," Dragon lies smoothly. "Why two glasses?"

"I thought your friend would be here. Figured you could share the bottle."

"Blake? No, Blake's not coming over tonight. She's got her head buried in a book."

"She?"

"Old habit," Dragon says. "Anyway, since you're already here and wine tastes better in company... would you care to join me for a glass, Rush?"

Rush stares at the Shaper for a moment. Then he asks, "What are you up to, Dragon?"

"Well, you'd have to come in to find out now, wouldn't you?" Dragon moves away from the door, and sets the bottle and glasses down on the desk. "Is there a corkscrew?"

"I've got it." Rush steps into the room. "You sit. I'll pour."

Dragon sits on the edge of the bed. "Could you do something about that, while you're at it?" it asks, gesturing toward the camera.

"Camera 3-B off," he says, and the red light blinks out. With a deft twist of the wrist, he pops the cork before secreting away the corkscrew in an inner pocket of his blazer. "You can try to shut the camera off yourself, but it won't work. Only Lorenzo and I have voice access."

Dragon watches as Rush pours the wine and hands it a glass, leaning against the desk with his own glass in hand. "You do that so well. Were you a waiter in a past life?"

"I wasn't anything in a past life."

Dragon wonders what that's supposed to mean, but instead it says, "Can I ask you a question, Rush?"

"You just did."

The Shaper reaches for the cigarettes and ashtray at

the foot of its bed, offering one to Rush, who declines it with a wave of his hand. "You know what I mean."

"I know."

Dragon tries again. "Do you ever take those sunglasses off?"

"I take them off when it's necessary."

"Would you take them off for me?"

"If you insist, Dragon," Rush says and removes them.

Dragon looks at those sweet, charming doll eyes, which change the whole impression of Rush's face from stone-hearted killer to deceptively innocent. "Must be tough to be a hard-assed secret service man with such pretty eyes like that."

"You have quite an attitude problem, you know."

"All attitude is influenced by circumstance," Dragon says.

Rush swirls the wine in his glass, tucking a loose curl behind his ear, then fixes his naked gaze on the Shaper. "Enough small talk. Tell me what you want."

The Shaper takes a long drag off its cigarette before letting the truth out. "I don't want those drugs. What they do, it's disgusting. It goes against my nature."

"I see," Rush says. "Now tell me what makes you think I would even *consider* letting you get out of that."

"I could make it worth your while," Dragon says.

"What could you possibly do for me that I can't make you do?"

A sultry burn comes to life in the Shaper's dark eyes as it sets down the cigarette and the glass, and places its fingers on the buttons of its shirt. Unbuttoned, the Shaper slips off the bed, standing before Rush, and seductively shrugs the shirt from its body.

"And what makes you think that I can't have that, too?" Rush asks.

"Not like you'd want it," the Shaper says, all matter-of-fact.

Rush is aware of the danger surrounding this Shaper. He places one hand on the Shaper's bare chest, over the perpetually taut nipple. The texture of the skin is like velvet. He watches the Shaper's face turn misty under his touch, but Rush knows that this is just an act. "You don't know what I want," Rush says.

"Are you sure?" Dragon asks, lifting its hands to Rush's face, which is smooth, as though recently shaven. It licks its dark lips slowly, its eyes heavy-lidded and smoldering, and takes one step closer to Rush. It then runs the tip of its tongue around the edges of Rush's lips. Rush closes his eyes as the Shaper kisses him hard, tongues entwining, dancing like serpents mating.

"Get on the bed," Rush orders, soft-voiced, when they part.

Dragon backs away and spreads it body down on the bed. Rush comes over, placing one knee on the side of its hip, his other foot still resting on the floor, and then he leans close to the Shaper. Rush smiles. The Shaper holds out its arms but Rush just shakes his head, gliding away.

"You don't know what I want," he says as he leaves, locking the door behind him.

⚢

Four weeks into the program, Blake says that it has a job.

"A job," Dragon says.

"Don't fucking repeat me," Blake snaps.

Dragon understands the reason behind Blake's tension. It's the fault of that chemical cocktail of which the agency is so fond, the speed drug. Blake said that it was like a big earthquake in your gut, with hell fire shooting out of it. But other than that, it wasn't so bad. Instead of shifting, you just kind of let yourself melt into the shape.

They haven't put me on it yet, Dragon said.

Any particular reason for that? Blake asked, smiling as if there were a nasty secret lurking somewhere behind its gentle mouth.

But not very gentle anymore. Blake, moving in and

out of its current shape, had changed. Still a woman, but it looked harder, stronger, blonder, taller. Subtle changes, really. *Could be a dozen different reasons,* Dragon replied, which was true. Since the failure of its seduction attempt, it has received no further sign of interest from Rush, even though they see each other on a daily basis. It has no idea what Rush is thinking.

"What kind of job?" Dragon asks now.

Blake crosses its stronger, slimmer arms over its chest. "I might as well say it, whether or not they want us to talk about it. You must have figured it out by now, anyway. The job is murder," Blake says, unblinking. "They've been training us to be assassins for the American government. Just like in the movies or something."

"Yeah," Dragon says strangely, thinking of Pride, "just like in the movies."

♀♂

After the release of Blake, Dragon found itself spending even more time with Rush in his office. It was a strange distraction, but a distraction nonetheless. The purpose of these meetings was for Rush "to get to know" the Shaper. It always had the atmosphere of an interrogation session, Rush firing off intrusive questions, and the Shaper answering them, sometimes truthfully and sometimes not, depending on its mood. Rush revealed a particular interest in the Shaper's home planet, its tribe and family life. The Shaper, on one of these nightly sessions, is answering, more or less honestly, questions regarding its first shape.

"What made you want to leave home?"

The Shaper shrugs. "Boredom, I guess. You know how we live. You know what we do."

Rush knows. The nomad tribes wander, keeping to themselves mostly, occasionally traveling to a Tiradian settlement where they mimic the Tiradians for awhile, like going on vacation. Then, once they had been "discovered" by other races, and with the eventual tourism that followed, the Shapers were presented with new forms to emulate, new places to go on "vacation" from themselves. Shapers, despite any apparent capacity for patience, are, by their nature, creatures that thrive on change.

"Then that human came. Nothing more fascinating than a human. You're so complex. Not physically, but the rest of it."

"So you just became that waiter and off you went."

Dragon shrugs. "There was more to it than that. I had to learn more than the shape. I also had to learn his mannerisms, who his friends were and how he acted towards them, how to drive the land cruiser, his fingerprints, and what a Tequila Sunrise was. And I only had five days in which to do it."

Rush snorts. "Bullshit," he says. "You must think I'm a fucking idiot if you expect me to believe you pulled that off. And in only five days."

Dragon remains silent. It feels a stirring in its stomach, an uncomfortable sensation that it does not recognize. It briefly wonders if it ate something disagreeable. Or if the organization had slipped some drug into its food – another possibility.

"Well?"

"Well, I'm here now, aren't I?" Dragon grumbles. "Does it really matter how?"

Rush drums his fingers on the desk, thinking. He leans over to the console and clicks off the voice recorder that always accompanies these meetings. "Go back to your room."

Dragon goes, always accompanied by Lorenzo or some other, nameless agent, back to its room. A nameless agent tonight, which is just as well, because Lorenzo tends to talk too much, always asking Dragon things like: Did you see the *Uffizi* in *Firenze?* What about the *Capella Sistina* in *Roma?* What about the *Basilica di San Marco* in *Venezia?* The *Palazzo Pubblico* in *Siena*, that's a pretty one, that *Campo* when it's lit up at night, have you seen it?

Dragon always answers with what little Italian it knows, *che bella, sì, mi piace,* and Lorenzo likes that. But Dragon is in no mood for conversation tonight, as the burning prickle in its stomach has intensified. Analyzing the sensation, it feels similar to heartburn, something that the Shaper had suffered briefly after its arrival on Earth as it adjusted to the new foods and their chemical residues. But the sensation is further down in its abdomen, too low to actually be heartburn. Also, it is feeling a little light-headed now, and there's a strange itch on its skin, where its shirt is tucked into its belt. It just wants to lie down.

Locked in its room, Dragon heads directly to the bathroom, where it unbuttons its shirt before the mirror with trembling fingers.

Climbing up its belly from below its belt up to the bottom of its ribcage is a red flush of skin, shiny like a first-degree burn. Dragon recognizes it immediately. There is no way that it could not recognize it, all the symptoms have been there for the past few days, it has just foolishly chosen to ignore them. Dragon has passed into its thirtieth Shaper year here in the confines of the agency building. Dragon, as Blake had pointed out, is at the age of conversion. And now the conversion has come, and Dragon is trapped in its unnatural shape, which could be very dangerous, if not fatal. Dragon does not know what to do. There has been, as far as it knows, no other situation where a Shaper in the mid-stages of conversion has been unable to shift back to its natural form. It is unprecedented.

Yet before Dragon can come to any conscious decision about this dilemma, a spasm of pain wracks its body and it falls to the bathroom floor, curled up in a fetal position, clutching its stomach in agony, unable to do anything.

⚥

Lorenzo sits at his desk, twirling a long coil of black

hair around his finger, thinking about his father who was a Communist. Lorenzo remembers when *they* came and took his father away, charging him with "subversive political thoughts" and "attempted radical disturbance." Which meant that Lorenzo's father would drink too much *grappa* with his *espresso* and then shoot off his mouth in the coffee bar about how Italy once was almost a Communist country after some war or other, but then the capitalist forces, with all their money, came in and changed that. Like how they did it again to create the United World Nation, buy everybody off. Bad enough that most of Western Europe had unified into a border-free union, why the whole world? What about culture? Tradition?

Lorenzo never saw his father again. He also knew that he had to get out of Syracuse which was already enduring the effects of the Mediterranean Renovation Program. Someone had decided that Sicily and parts of what used to be Greece should be made into a vacation resort for the important and wealthy. Lorenzo had entertained no dreams about growing up to be a colorful local. He was better than that. It was with hard work and luck that he ended up in the agency, and had made something of his life. *We're going to drill that Italian pride out of you, boy,* they'd said in training. They hadn't, of course, but Lorenzo let them think they had. Lorenzo still had his dreams. He wanted to change the system from the inside.

Lorenzo sits at his desk, entertaining his Communist thoughts, feeling useless. He often suffers moments like this, when he is forced to handle some petty task. His task at the moment is to follow Blake's movements via the tracking implant as it makes its way towards London. Except that it isn't Blake anymore; now the Shaper is Elisabeth Garibaldi, an identity chosen by Lorenzo himself. The allusion to the twentieth century Italian revolutionary did not slip past Rush, but he'd let the name slide.

Blake is right on course. Lorenzo gets up from his desk, stretches, decides to get a cup of coffee. He walks down the hallway, greets the night man at the main checkpoint, and reaches for the coffee pot. "How's it going?" Lorenzo asks, pouring.

"Quiet."

Lorenzo wanders over to the desk and looks at the monitor screens. His eye lingers on 3-B. "What's going on there?"

The night man shrugs. "Our friend's a little camera shy. Spends hours in the john. Takes a two hour bath, every night, like clockwork."

Lorenzo glances at his watch. It is ten past one. "How long has it been in there?"

"Don't know," says the night man, but, hearing the suspicion in Lorenzo's voice, he is already rewinding the recording. The digital readout on the bottom of the screen blinks. 22:04. Just over three hours ago.

"Something's wrong," Lorenzo says, his intuition suddenly cranked up to full volume. "Get me two men, armed and loaded, at the door," he orders. "I'm going in."

"Damn," Lorenzo murmurs at the door of the bathroom.

"What the hell is wrong with it?" someone says.

"It's not a trick, is it?" someone else says.

"I don't know," Lorenzo replies. "It's real enough to be a problem. You – pick it up."

One of the agents holsters his Disabler and leans over the Shaper who is still curled up on the floor, its body jerking violently with spasms, its breathing shallow, skin flushed a rose color, eyes rolled back in its head, moaning occasionally. The Shaper is dying.

The agent who touched the Shaper jumps back. "Christ! It's hotter than a goddamn furnace."

Lorenzo then notices how hot the room is, and that the mirror is filmed over with steam. "I don't give a fuck about that," he snaps. "Just get the damn thing on the bed. Come on."

The agent and Lorenzo pick up the Shaper, so much dead weight, and Lorenzo feels its incredible fever, and knows that this is serious. Too serious. He shoots a glance at the other agent. "Get Rush," he orders. "Now."

☿

Something wakes Rush in the middle of the night. Eyes hazy, he glances at the screen by his bed. Just after one in the morning. *What was it?* The tail end of a dream maybe. He tries to grab onto the dream before it vanishes.

There. A fleeting image. Another Shaper dream, this time of a tribe dancing around a bonfire. And, in this dream, Rush was one of them, and Dragon was there. Although it looked like any other Shaper, Rush recognized it, and Dragon came to him, and then – *Then what?* But the image is gone. *No matter.* Rush, still hazy, decides to roll over and go back to sleep. All else in his apartment loft is quiet.

But as soon as he rolls over onto his chest, he realizes that it was something else that woke him, not the dream. The silk sheets are rubbing his skin in a most irritating manner. He bolts up in bed, turns on the light, and lifts the sheet away from his body. He contemplates the red flush like a rash which covers the lower half of his abdomen and then he swears. "That fucking Shaper," he says.

He is already awake and dressed when he receives the call. The agent's taut face appears on the screen, apologizing for the disturbance but something is wrong, and Lorenzo –

Rush cuts him off abruptly. "Put Lorenzo online."

The picture flips and now Rush is looking at Lorenzo and the other agent and the Shaper dying on the bed. "Lorenzo."

Lorenzo glances up at the camera fixed in the corner of the room. "What do I do, Rush?"

"I'm deactivating the disc," Rush says. "All you have

to do is *watch* it. Don't take one fucking eyeball off it. Got it?"

"Got it."

Rush punches in the proper codes, waits, checks the screen to see if the Shaper will shift back to its natural form. Nothing happens. "It's too far gone," Rush mutters to himself.

"What, boss?" Lorenzo asks without moving his eyes from the Shaper.

"You have to sedate it. An ampule of morphine, understand? I'm on my way in."

"Understood," Lorenzo says. "Rush? What the hell's wrong with it?"

"The conversion," Rush says, now aware of the significance of the term. "That Shaper has just come into sexual maturity."

Lorenzo now turns his face to the camera in surprise. "What?"

"It's in heat," Rush says, and breaks the connection.

♂

The morphine is coursing nicely through the Shaper's system by the time Rush arrives. Its breathing has become more regular and its fever has dropped by a few degrees. If he were of a different frame of mind at the moment, Lorenzo would have noticed that Rush looks quite unlike his usual self. Instead of the perpetual dark suit, he looks like a "Gap" advertisement in a pair of jeans and a loose cotton pullover. Also, not only are the sunglasses missing, but his hair is falling in loose spirals down around his shoulders, freed from its usual severe ponytail. Rush looks like a corn-fed boy straight out of Wyoming, fresh and naïve.

"What the hell do you mean, 'it's in heat'?" Lorenzo asks as Rush enters.

Rush approaches the bed. "Do you know how big Shapers make little Shapers?"

"When two of them are fertile, one impregnates the other. About five months later, it gives birth," Lorenzo says quickly, with the flat tone of someone reciting from memory. "Are you saying that our Shaper is going to die because it needs to give birth?"

"No," Rush says. "Get up." Lorenzo rises, and Rush takes the chair by the Shaper's bed. "What I'm saying is that this is our Shaper's first quickening, which means it's the giver, not the receiver. Which means it's been growing a haploid cell in its reproductive organ – in its uterus, if that's what you want to call it – but it's having a problem with the shape. It has to go back to its natural form in order to push the cell out, whether or not there's another Shaper to receive it."

"What if there's no other Shaper around?" Lorenzo asks, meaning: *We've got no other Shaper, what do we do now?*

"There usually is. They usually come into heat as a group, every five years or so. In unusual circumstances, where the timing is off, whatever Shaper closest to it will then also come into heat prematurely, as long as it has quickened in the past, which makes Blake useless – it's too young – what fucking shit." Rush stares at the Shaper, trying to pull his thoughts together. But Rush's mind is hazy, light, and thinking is growing steadily more difficult. It takes great effort to maintain control. "It's too late, anyway – there weren't any other Shapers around at the first stages that would have been forced into – *uh* – heat – God fucking *damn* it–"

"Rush?"

Rush rubs at his forehead, which is suddenly hot. "Fuck. Stupid Shapers. You don't know how strong the impulse to reproduce is in these Shapers – worse than fucking animals – survival of the species –" Rush stumbles over his words. "It might die –"

"Are you okay, Rush?" Lorenzo asks, seeing his boss' expression, glassy-eyed, mouth slack, distant. *Porca miseria*, Lorenzo thinks, *is Rush in love with the Shaper?*

Rush's composure returns and he looks at Lorenzo. "Yeah, I'm just… distracted."

"Yeah," Lorenzo mumbles.

"All right," Rush says. "You three – get out. I'll handle this."

That is more like the Rush that Lorenzo knows. He nods his head and they go, leaving Rush alone with the Shaper. "Camera 3-B off," he orders, and then leans closer to the Shaper. "Dragon," he says. There is no response. "Dragon." Nothing. "Goddamn it, Dragon, you stupid fuck, I'm not going to let you die!"

Dragon's eyelids flutter and its eyes roll back into place. Its voice is slow and heavy from the rush of morphine. "Enough," it says.

"No," Rush says emphatically.

"Child," Dragon murmurs.

"Look at me." Rush's voice quivers, fainter now. He can feel himself losing words, whole languages, ideals, philosophies, all intellect, all identity. He is losing not only speech but the thoughts behind it, reason, logic and rationale. It is all slipping away despite his efforts to control it. *Crazy*, he thinks, as he pulls the shirt over his head. His body is a crackling wire of unbridled *need, need, need*. He staggers to his feet, unbuckling his jeans. The skin of his belly is red and hot, like a first-degree burn, spreading from his groin to the bottom of his ribcage.

Dragon looks at Rush. "You…" it says as Rush comes to the bed and climbs over the Shaper, taking it by the shoulders. Dragon feels the heat rising off Rush's skin, and it *knows*. "You fuckin' bastard," it slurs.

"Shift damn you!" Rush screams, his eyes turning black, as though the pupils were oozing out from the center and devouring the hazel of his irises. It is the last coherent human sound that Rush makes because blind primal instinct has taken over, obliterating all consciousness with the all-consuming fire of the *need, need, need*. Crouched naked over Dragon's body, Dragon sees those eyes darkening, feels the thunder of Rush's heart as if it were its own pulse, and watches in awe as Rush shifts.

I should have known, Dragon thinks, but then its own instinct is like an electrifying explosion, nerves on fire, and it, too, loses the ability to think, and it, too, shifts, falling into the arms of the other Shaper.

Lorenzo returns to his office. He has forgotten all about that coffee. He must admit that he is a bit shaken. He wonders what got into Rush. A scowl distorts his fine Italian brow. *If Rush is indeed in love with the Shaper –*

He glances at his dead monitor. He should just continue to track Blake, after all, that is his job. If he does anything else, he could lose his job. He sits very still, entrenched in his internal debate. Curiosity wins out. He turns on the monitor and calls up room 3-B. Blank. Rush must have turned the camera off. That seems a little unusual to Lorenzo, especially given the circumstances. "Replay film camera 3-B, thirty seconds," he says. He watches the last thirty seconds of recorded film, which shows Rush ordering the agents to leave the room. The first thing that Rush did once they had left the room was to shut down the camera.

Lorenzo hesitates a moment, considers his options, then gives the voice command. "Camera 3-B on," he says.

PART 3
KA'RAEL

The whore appears out of the shadows with her painted lips and the obligatory shake of her hips. "Hey, you, pretty boy," she says.

The person, to whom she has just called out, stops in his ramble down the dusky New York City street and regards her curiously. In the background a dog barks and men shout over a perpetual police siren hum. Farther than that, there is sporadic gunfire, faint with the distance, like firecrackers popping.

She sashays over to him. Closer, he can see the garish mask of paint over the faded features of a once exotic beauty. Her eyes are less than lucid, but her voice is flint sharp. "What's a nice boy like you doing in a place like this? Aren't you scared?"

He shakes his head. He is not surprised by her questions, knowing well how he appears. His slim frame and slight stature give him an air of frailty, his beardless, sloping face is youthfully sweet, and his hair falls down around his thin shoulders in golden waves, fine and silky like the locks of a child. Neon light paints circus-colored streaks into that fine honey hair while the shadows lap hollows under the bird-like bones.

"What's your name?" she asks.

He fixes her for a moment with large, green eyes, eyes that are far too old and wise for such a young face. "Ka'rael," he replies.

"Ka'rael... strange name for a strange boy," she decides.

He adjusts the purple velvet cloak which hangs by a

cord at his too long, too pale throat. "What is your name?"

"Doesn't really matter, does it?" she says, laughing, but the hard edge in her voice betrays the flippancy of the remark. "People around here call me Lady Zorba because my father was Greek."

"But that is not your name," Ka'rael points out gently.

"A name doesn't mean a thing."

He smiles kindly, a gesture which transforms his thin mouth into something beautiful. "But, I'm afraid, that is where you are mistaken. To know the true name of a thing gives the power to control it. Words shape worlds, give context and define, and to categorize is dangerously misleading. Truth is obscured when men try to put nature into words. Names define, but at the same time they limit the perspective, taint the meaning, and confine the truth instead of letting the truth be unbound, as it should be. Absolute truth, like all things of great beauty, cannot be placed into words without being distorted, or destroyed."

His eyes shine.

"Fuck, hold on," Lady Zorba interjects. "I didn't ask for some philosophical mumbo jumbo. I knew you were strange, but you're some kind of poetic strange, or something. Shit, boy. You *are* in the wrong neighborhood."

"And so are you," he says softly, so softly that she is unsure for a moment that he even spoke at all.

"Fuck you, freak," she says. "Enough of this bullshit. Get the hell out of here, go back to Nebraska or Mars or wherever the hell you came from." She steps away, scanning the dusk for prospective clients, but there is no one promising in view. No cars with Jersey plates with rich suburban boys looking for a good time. She glances back at the boy who has not moved an inch, still regarding her with the same profound and luminous look. "What the hell are you waiting for?" she asks sullenly.

"For you," he says.

She laughs again. "Shit, I'm old enough to be your aunt or something. How old are you?"

He smiles again with that profoundly beautiful smile. "Old enough."

She stuffs her hands into the pockets of her tattered leather jacket, staring at him. "You got any money?"

"I have money," he says and holds out his hand to her. "Come with me."

Strange he may be, but dangerous he is not, Lady Zorba assesses. Indeed, despite their surroundings, his presence radiates a strange sort of calm, like the eye of a storm. Plus, with business being so slow, it wasn't as if any better offers were coming her way tonight. "Oh, what the hell," she says, and takes his hand.

☿

Rush leans back in his chair, regarding the Shaper standing before him. The shape is different, not nearly as beautiful, but still tall and strong and lean. The black hair is groomed and respectably short, nose narrow, lips pale and full, and the eyes are gray and cold like steel. Rush has seen those particular eyes before.

"Congratulations on finishing your training, Dragon," Rush says and then removes a thin, black tablet from within his desk, sliding it towards the Shaper. "This is your first job. Consider it a test. After the job is completed, you erase the file. Every trace of it. Do you understand?"

The Shaper puts on a wry smile for Rush's benefit, stretching out one long, white hand to pick up the netbook. "I understand."

"Good." Rush watches Dragon as it turns on the machine, touches the screen, and begins scanning the file. "All the information is there: the who, what, where and how. The why is not important to you."

The Shaper's thick brows furrow as it reads. It glances at Rush. "You can't be serious," it says.

"But I am," Rush says. "Regardless of whatever you think happened between us, know that failure of this test will result in termination of your employment. And you know what that means."

The images of the cleansing that Dragon had witnessed on the video have never wandered far from the forefront of its mind. It knows that it has no other choice. "Let's get to work then, shall we?" it says.

♂

When Lady Zorba enters Ka'rael's room, she starts to suspect that the boy does not actually have sufficient funds for this transaction and that she's just wasting her time, and, after all, in her line of work, time is money.

Ka'rael has a room in one of those rundown, pay-by-the-week hotels where the toilet is at the far end of the hall. The room is barren and somewhat depressing, cracked plaster walls with the last lime-green paint job peeking through the cream-colored overcoat. The only visible possessions are some clothes piled shapelessly on a chair in the corner of the room, and a small, stone mosaic adhered to the wall. Upon closer inspection, Lady Zorba sees that the square mosaic is a depiction of the Annunciation, the kind that you can buy from any sidewalk vendor, except that it is beautifully executed. The angel seems to be glowing, and Mary's expression seems genuine and blessed, unlike in so many other reproductions in stone.

"Are you religious or something?" she asks. The religious fanatics, in her experience, are always the hardest to handle.

"Not in the sense that you mean," Ka'rael says.

She turns. "You're not involved in one of those freaky new cults, are you?"

He shakes his golden head.

"You sure you've got the money?"

"Would you like to see it?"

"I only take payment in advance."

He reaches into the pocket of his torn jeans and pulls out a wad of paper currency, holding it out. "Is your time worth that?"

She takes the money, counts it quickly. "What do you want me to do?" she asks, expecting something unusual for such a large sum. She is now starting to suspect that she might have misjudged the boy – maybe he *is* one of those religious freaks, after all.

"Come lie on the bed," he says gently. She takes off her jacket while he sits down, rearranging the pillows for her head. Once she has stretched out, he says, "Close your eyes, child."

She wants to laugh at this boy calling her a child, but, for what he is paying, she will let him call her whatever he likes. She closes her eyes. After a moment, she notices that she feels strangely peaceful, as though his eye-of-the-storm aura of tranquility has spread out to envelop her. She can't remember the last time she felt so calm except when she first started shooting up. *How long ago was that?* She can't even remember.

Ka'rael leans over her to place his hands on her head. He strokes her dark hair, brushing it back from her forehead. "There's no need to worry," he says.

She sinks further into the sensation of tranquility, drifting like a feather on sluggish water. "I still think you're a strange boy," she murmurs.

What she does not know is that the boy stroking her head so gently is not a boy. Though Ka'rael is often mistaken for a feminine man or a masculine woman, he is neither. Sometimes, such misperceptions lead to trouble, as if Ka'rael's intention had been to "trick" people. Yet to those who prefer their sexes less defined, Ka'rael is often considered beautiful. In its travels, however, Ka'rael has encountered very few souls, particularly in the less cosmopolitan places on Earth, who fall into the latter category. Most humans prefer things to be black and white. Ka'rael is a shade of gray.

Ka'rael strokes the crook of her arm which is scarred by needle marks. "Drugs are bad for you," it says to her, all the while bathing her with the serenity of its being.

Lady Zorba is somewhere else now, deep within herself where Ka'rael has taken her. "I know," she says.

"It will kill you if you don't stop."

"I don't deserve to live." Her answer is real; while in this trance, she cannot speak a lie.

Ka'rael has found the fear that it needs. In the blink of an eye, consciousness separates from body with no other sound than the squeak of a rusty bedspring as its discarded flesh falls to the bed.

Ka'rael plunges into the darkest recesses of the whore's mind. At an opportune moment, it opens its wings to catch the air, slowing its descent, and begins its search. Her inner landscape is a night sky full of distant stars and ancient gods. Below, a raging torrent of a river threads through ruins of toppled pantheons and fields of black briars laced with red poppies and roses. Ka'rael swoops down, letting itself be carried on a rapid wind until it finds the first knot, a bitter snarl of rusted barbed wire. Ka'rael tugs and jerks on the knot with all its strength. It creaks and splinters, sending glittery brown dust up into the air, momentarily obliterating all the stars. A dozen black, demon-like creatures lurking behind the wire break free of the dark. Ka'rael withdraws its sword which burns with blue flames and slays them all.

Turning, it calls out to her.

It speaks her true name.

"Your children need you," it says.

In the shabby hotel room, tears spill out from beneath Lady Zorba's closed eyes. "My children," she murmurs, her voice echoing in the empty room.

Ka'rael surveys the battlefield. There, in a dark corner, something else slithers. Ka'rael recognizes it as the fear. It courageously draws the monster out and battles once again with the flaming sword. The monster slain, Ka'rael sheathes its weapon and scans the horizon, but it does not venture farther into the depths. There is danger once a certain boundary is crossed, and, instinctively, it recognizes where that boundary lies. But it knows that it has done good work by the time the battle with the dark forces within the prostitute is won, and Ka'rael withdraws carefully. The human mind is a fragile thing – Ka'rael has learned that, too – and to alter its state incautiously would only risk causing anguish, insanity, or death.

Then it is back in the material plane, consciousness rehoused in fatigued flesh, lying on the bed with the prostitute's head still in its hands. It releases her from the trance in such a way that she will not remember what has happened.

She opens her eyes and looks at the creature above her.

"You fell asleep," it says. Then it adds, "It is late and you are tired. You should go home."

"Home," she repeats. Her mind is strangely lucid, despite having just woken. She is thinking about her children, how they need her. What the hell is she doing with her life? *It's not too late to change things, is it?* She's not too old, she could go back to school, get an education, a day job even. Her children could have a real life, a better chance. Suddenly, inexplicably, they are the most important thing in her life. She rises from the bed and then fumbles in her pocket. "I can't keep all this money," she says. "I didn't do anything to earn it."

Again its lips form the odd, beatific smile. "No, you did earn it. I said I would pay you for your time."

She hesitates and then pockets the money, readying herself to leave. "Well," she says, "thank you," but it isn't about the money, really. She's not exactly sure why she feels so grateful; she just does. Once she is gone and Ka'rael has bolted the door behind her, it lays down upon the bed still warm from her body, and falls into a state that resembles deep, dreamless sleep.

A dozen agents clutch a dozen coffee cups and at least a half dozen cigarettes, waiting for the meeting to commence. They would be nervous if they did not possess nerves of steel, because it is rare that Rush convenes a meeting. Of course, due to the private nature of both Rush and the agency, the purpose of the meeting is a mystery.

Except one of the agents has a noticable case of the jitters, but it has nothing to do with the gathering itself. It has to do with Rush, the man who is not actually a man but a Shaper. Lorenzo is the only agent in the organization who knows the truth. As he sits at the end of the table, his mind wanders back to what he saw when he turned on camera 3-B.

He saw two brown-skinned Shaper bodies entwining, the skin from their abdomens opening up and spreading back, blooming wide like otherworldly orchids, flowers from hell. Then they came together, bellies merging, and one of them was howling like an injured dog or something, Dragon maybe – it was hard to determine which one was which at that point – and Lorenzo could not tell if the Shaper was in pain or ecstasy or both. Jesus, it was weird. And now he is sitting here, slightly agitated because five days ago he had placed a call to a secret branch of the DOD, to the guys who are *really* in charge of the Shaper Rehabilitation Program, and so far nothing has happened beyond the order that Lorenzo act as if everything were normal. So Lorenzo has pretended, and everything has continued as normally as it ever did before the call. Except that every time Lorenzo looks at Rush, all he can think of is how Rush shifted and then got fucked by that other Shaper, and he wonders if Rush has some little Shaper growing in his body. In his *uterus,* for Christ's sake. *What will happen when the child starts to show? It will show, won't it?*

Lorenzo is torn from his mental wanderings at the appearance of Rush, followed by the new, "improved" Dragon. Lorenzo is not surprised that Rush never lets the Shaper out of his sight, all things considered. Rush takes his place at the head of the table opposite Lorenzo while the Shaper lingers by the door, lacking, as usual, a readable expression.

"Let's get down to business," Rush says. "I've called you here today because you are my most trusted men. As you know, trust is not something easily earned in our profession. But I rely on the discretion and the loyalty which each of you have demonstrated in the past. So I feel confident enough to keep you informed of any problems which arise within the agency." Rush pauses, gauging for reactions. No one seems too comfortable with the word *problems.*

"Your job is to follow orders," Rush continues. "Obedience is not negotiable. So when one of my own agents disobeys orders and commits an act of conspiracy against me, then I am permitted to dole out the proper reprimand at my own discretion."

Rush adjusts his mirrored shades as he nods at the Shaper. Eyes but not heads swivel towards the back of the room. Lorenzo is suddenly numb with fear and cannot will himself to turn and look at the Shaper standing behind him.

Dragon, at Rush's signal, with one fluid movement, reaches into its jacket pocket and pulls out a .44 snub-nosed Magnum and places the mouth of it against the back of Lorenzo's head. In the deafening silence of the room, the cocking of the weapon sounds like a bomb detonating.

Lorenzo stops breathing, but his eyes are imploring Rush. Meanwhile, Dragon is wishing that it were somewhere else, anywhere but here. It doesn't want to shoot anybody, not Lorenzo, hell, it almost even likes Lorenzo.

Rush smiles coldly at Lorenzo, a powerful, condescending smile that would shame the devil. "One thing, Lorenzo," Rush says. "You didn't tell them anything that they weren't already aware of. Why do you think they gave me this job? They *knew,* Lorenzo, believe me, they *knew.*" With that said, Rush rises from the table and turns his back.

Dragon pulls the trigger of the gun and blows

Lorenzo's brains out from one end of the table to the other. Nobody flinches, nobody says a word. The assassin then holsters its gun and turns away in silence.

♂

Rush peruses the file detailing Dragon's next job on his desk monitor. It should not be too difficult to track down the terrorist whose name appears in the document, yet it is obvious that the FBI is having difficulty or the file would not be in Rush's private in-box.

The man in the file, Jack Dunsmore, has skillfully eluded the Feds for some time now. A low-profile criminal, Dunsmore's MO is to commit acts of terrorism via intricate and advanced hacking techniques. Any time that a construction intended for a social program – drug rehabilitation, housing for the homeless, and similar programs – is planned, Dunsmore infiltrates the system and alters the blueprints. Subtle, nearly undetectable alterations that eventually cause the building to collapse on its unsteady foundations. Many innocent people have been killed and now the government must act, although Rush speculates that the government is more concerned over the capital losses than the human ones.

Also, lately, Dunsmore has caused some problems inside the government network, a little too close to the President to be comfortable. Whether Dunsmore is trying to harm the infrastructure of the government – or just prove that he can – is also subject to Rush's speculation. Either way, the man is a problem that must be resolved.

It took a long time to track down Dunsmore's headquarters but they were eventually traced to New York City. The first undercover agent sent in to investigate never came back out. Later it was discovered that the reason why the agent never came out was because the agent had joined Dunsmore's small, yet highly-skilled task force. It was also discovered that the agent had not become a traitor by choice. For his team Dunsmore had managed to procure a once-famous biochemist whose specialized field of study was mind control. So the only way that the Feds could reach the man himself was to send in someone who had no mind.

At least someone with no *human* mind.

While Rush is recording notes in the margins of the file, he receives a red flag from NewsWatch, a governmental newsfeed linked to every media publisher on the planet. Rush relies heavily on the service, and filters the feed for any information related to anything resembling possible alien activity. He stops recording to glance over the message. It is from a small tabloid out of New York City. He contemplates the article for a moment, but he is doubtful about the validity of the article's claims, as it is from a tabloid. *Still,* he muses, *I am sending Dragon to New York. Maybe two birds with one stone.*

Rush rises from his desk, feeling surprisingly good. There is a slight movement within his body, in his reproductive organ – or his uterus, as it has been called, as it is similar to the human female organ. He feels stronger and more powerful than he has ever felt before.

He crosses the room to the larger screen on the wall and calls up the Archives. In a moment he has retrieved the file on the Shaman that has been gathering the proverbial dust for three years. Many scores of years ago, the word Shaman used to denote a medicine man, but the name had been adapted to describe a certain race from a small planet off the grid, so unknown that they would seem like fiction to the average man – just like Shapers. But this Shaman is real; Rush has seen it with his own eyes, touched it with his own hands. Unfortunately, the agency had underestimated its ability and it managed to escape, then disappear without a trace.

Rush returns to his desk, looking at the files side by side on his monitor. He decides that he will hand them both over to the Shaper, making Dunsmore high priority, of course, before investigating the matter of the Shaman. Rush calls for Dragon so that he can give it its first two assignments outside the agency's complex. Rush could never forget that strange creature, like anyone else who had ever met it, whether they knew what it was or not. *What was its name?* In the quiet moment before the Shaper's arrival, the name of the Shaman springs like the words of a familiar song to Rush's lips. "Ka'rael," he says.

♂

"Right there," the editor says, pointing at the middle of the screen. "We don't know what that is."

"Pour me another shot of that, will you?" says the man sitting at the back table. Kincaid O'Bryan tilts the bourbon bottle to refill his friend's plastic cup.

Max Pride leans closer to the screen as though it would make the jumble of code any clearer. Instead, the letters and symbols start to blur. "What the fuck did that *baka* bitch do?"

The editor sighs and mutters irately, "Max, don't get yourself so damned worked up."

He allows his editor to speak to him in that tone. He would let her do anything. After all, she is his wife. "Ophelia, I have every right to get worked up."

She sighs again. She does not want to argue.

"There isn't anyone in the whole department who can fix this?"

"I told you already," Ophelia says. "Rob tried to run a copy and the whole thing fell apart. There is no way that we can edit those scenes without losing half the footage. The film's already been half-encoded."

Pride tries to not lose his patience, but it is growing more difficult by the minute. "Did anyone call in that CGI specialist from California yet?"

"*Hai*," Kincaid says, "but he's under contract with Spielberg Productions and won't be available for three weeks. And you know how those Spielberg people are."

"Bastards," Max says. "Of course, a legally fucking binding contract didn't stop our FX computer wiz from running out and leaving this fucking mess."

Kincaid's friend raises a dark eyebrow. "Say, 'caid, isn't it that girl you were telling me about? The one who just vanished, leaving no trace of anything except her clothes? Do you think she bailed buck naked?"

"*Nanda? Ie,* I don't think so," Kincaid says. "There were a few things missing from the wardrobe, but they were men's clothes. Large ones. And that night she disappeared, the whole wardrobe department was in shambles, then the door was completely busted, and all the alarms going off..." His voice trails off, and he stares into his cup. "Sounds like foul play to me."

"Hey," says his friend, "maybe she was like a Shaper or something and those production guys were actually Secret Service men trying to catch her."

Kincaid regards him with his watery eye, and very seriously tells him that he could be right.

Pride shoots the men a nasty look. "Who are you, anyway?"

"Jeremy Butkins," replies the dark man.

"Oh," Pride says as cold as ice. "The porn star with the fifteen inch dick."

"That's right," Jeremy says smoothly. "Would you like to see it?"

"Hell no, but I would like the both of you to shut the fuck up," Pride says. He looks at his wife who shrugs help-lessly at him, and then at the screen again. "Shit, I'd give a million credits to see Dahlia right now so I could make her finish this film..." he says thoughtfully, "*then* I'd kill her."

The irony that it is climbing in through a warehouse window is not lost on Dragon. Of course it is aware that this is not Lion Productions, instead it is Jack Dunsmore's fortress, and that alone should have warned Dragon that the level of security would be far greater. An alarm is tripped silently and the men are upon the Shaper in no time.

They slap Dragon around a little, not to hurt so much as to scare. They relieve Dragon of its gun and the fake FBI badge with which it has been supplied for the occasion. The questions come next. Dragon refuses to reveal any more than its name and security number, both of which are as valid as the badge. For its noncompliance it receives a sharp jab in the gut. Dragon falls to its knees, gasping for air. The three men laugh and one of them lights a cigarette, the moonlight flashing off the brass lighter as his yellowed thumb flicks the wheel. He takes a drag off the cigarette and then says, "Shoot him."

Dragon grits its teeth and feels the bee sting stab of a needle in its exposed neck. It expected this and knows what to do. It lets its body sag a little as if the drug were having an effect. The act is clearly a credible one, for they seize the Shaper, dragging it across the floor by its arms through the warehouse and down into the basement. It keeps its eyes half-closed, watching through the slits, memorizing the path they take through the labyrinth.

Soon Dragon is half-looking at Dunsmore, a long-faced thin man who sits in an armchair with a gun balanced on one knee. One of the men murmurs into his boss's ear.

Dunsmore leans closer to the Shaper. "David Goddard," he says, the name on the badge. Dragon lifts its head, keeping its expression dull and vacant, bovine. The perfect deception. "Can you hear me, David?"

Keeping its voice as monotonous as its expression, Dragon replies. "Yes."

"Who are you working for, David?"

"Federal Bureau of Investigations, Special Forces Division."

"And what is your mission, David?"

"To apprehend, dead or alive, one man known as Jack Dunsmore."

Dunsmore laughs as though he has just heard a funny joke. "No, David Goddard, that is not your mission.

Your mission is to protect Dunsmore."

"Protect Dunsmore…"

"You would even give your life to protect Dunsmore."

"Protect Dunsmore…"

"Why, you even worship Dunsmore. You think that he's your own personal Messiah. As the saying goes, 'Dunsmore does more.' Go ahead and say it, David, it will make you feel good. Dunsmore does more."

"Dunsmore does more," the Shaper repeats.

Dunsmore laughs again. "That was too easy," he says to the others. "These government boys are fresh off their mammas' tits." The other men laugh. "One of these days I might get a challenge if I'm lucky."

Now is the moment. Dragon sees that Dunsmore is distracted. Also, the others are now more at ease, it can sense that from them. Dragon hopes that no one has a weapon pointed at its back as it suddenly lunges and snatches up the gun resting on Dunsmore's knee.

It happens in one decisive, fluid moment, as by its training: the long Shaper arm reaching forward, the gun in its hand, turning over, grip falling into open palm and squeeze the trigger, once, twice, into Dunsmore's chest, then the Shaper rolls away, to the side of the chair and fixes the men in its sights, arm already extended and firing. Gunfire fills the air with the thick, bitter odor of hot metal friction and gunpowder mixed with the brass smell of blood. Dragon takes a hit in the chest but manages to keep firing, picking them off one at a time, rapid yet efficient, never panicking, never feeling fear. Not feeling anything.

Dragon stands, surveying the corpses only briefly because it knows that if it wants to survive, it has to get out of there before more men arrive. A cough rattles some blood out of the Shaper's throat, but the pain is not raging yet, so, ignoring the wound, it lets itself melt out of the Goddard shape. Gun in hand, Dragon is then standing at the door, facing the men drawn by the shots fired only a few minutes before.

"Dunsmore," one of them is asking the Shaper, "are you okay?"

"I'm fine," replies the Shaper in Dunsmore's voice. "There was an intruder on the premises that I had to take care of."

"Boss, you're bleeding," he says. "Christ, were you hit?"

"I told you I'm fine," Dragon says.

Then the man leans closer, staring intently at the Shaper's eye. "Jesus, boss, there's something wrong with your face."

Dragon knows, without needing a mirror, that what is "wrong" with its face is the twitch. The shape is shaky because the agency's chemical cocktail makes it difficult to hold the shape under normal circumstances, and the pain from the bullet wound in its chest is increasingly distracting. Dragon makes a decision. There seems to be no other way out of the room than through this door, and the Shaper is convinced that it has to get out of there or it's dead, so it lifts Dunsmore's gun to the face of the man before him and fires quickly before anyone else can react. The Shaper silently prays like it has only prayed one time before, on the night that the moon turned the color of blood.

♂

"Here you go, sweetie," the waitress says as she delivers the requested sweet roll.

Ka'rael thanks her and returns to reading *The New York Times*. No news must be good news because all of the news is bad news. It doesn't understand why the human mind hungers after and savors all the horror, pain and tragedy in the world. No wonder why his people found humans so disagreeable. The Shaman shuts off the screen in the counter. It is thinking about its people now, something that it does not do very often.

They are no longer my people, it thinks. *I have no people. I am alone.*

But knowing it is alone and feeling lonely are two different things. Ka'rael does not feel lonely. It is surrounded by humans, disagreeable as they are, in this greasy diner to which it comes every day. If the Shaman lets its mind drift – extending past the boundaries of its own consciousness, just a little – it can skim the surface of their thoughts. Collectively, the thoughts of the people in the diner pool together into an incoherent mire of brain noise. Ka'rael can pick out some thoughts, bits and pieces jutting out of the mental airwaves.

The man beside it is thinking about the job he has just finished, he did good work, he is satisfied. If only the hours were shorter and the pay a hell of a lot better.

The girl in the corner gives off a high buzz of emotional static, waiting for a boy she likes to come in through the door. She is excited and nervous, worried about how she looks, worried that he might not come.

The woman behind him is thinking about the psychic reading she just had, and how amazing it was that the handsome psychic had told her things about herself that he couldn't possibly have known, like he was looking into her mind.

Ka'rael, amused, smiles to itself. It is still relaxed and happy in this loose state of open consciousness when a bolt of pain smashes into its head like a sledgehammer. Ka'rael jerks on the bar stool, grabbing onto the counter to keep itself steady. It searches for the source of the pain but it is not coming from inside the building. The source is somewhere outside.

Hastily it pays the bill and adjusts the Greek fisherman's cap over its golden locks as it steps outside the door. As it moves down the street, the terrible pain in its head increases. It has to stop for a moment to adjust its consciousness – like tuning the frequency of a radio – before it continues. The Shaman does not know what it will do when it locates the source of this suffering, just like it did not know that it was going to explore the prostitute's internal landscape until it happened. It just follows its instincts.

There, up ahead, it spies a man in a dark trench coat, with short, black hair and a pale face, half-stumbling through the street while clutching his chest with one hand. Ka'rael moves quickly but does not catch up with the man. Ka'rael, in its own special way, is listening to the man. It can hear the scattered thoughts flying off him like water droplets from a dog shaking its rain-drenched coat.

Didn't want... you cold-hearted, no heart bastard son of a... so much blood... the moon... the gun was cold... all of them dead... the child... must not think about it... no choice... didn't want to kill them... run away... I want to go home... sick chemicals... bad shift... fuckfuckfuckbloodlungs painpainPAIN... Blakeyouwere right whereare you now...

As the man ducks into a building, Ka'rael stops and lingers on the corner. It feels strongly for the stranger, so much pain and sorrow, but it hesitates to follow. There is something extremely dark and ominous brewing within that man, and Ka'rael is uncertain if it is really prepared to take a look. Its mouth tightens, eyes narrow. *I cannot go where I am not invited*, it tells itself to convince itself, then it turns and retreats back down the street whence it came.

With thoughts thundering like skittish horses, Dragon, hands shaking, reaches out to turn on the screen by its bed. It tears open the front of its blood-soaked shirt, pressing its hand to the wound which is now throbbing wildly. Rush's face flashes on the screen. "Dragon. Report."

"I've been hit," Dragon says.

"And Dunsmore?"

"Taken care of... fuck, Rush, I've been fucking shot!"

Rush surveys the situation with his usual calm. "You

can handle it," he says, almost an order. "Stop the bleeding."

Dragon leans back against the headboard, pressing
its hand firmly against the hole above its right breast.

"Where's the bullet?" Rush asks.

"Went through."

"Good. Now tell me what was hit."

"Lung," Dragon sputters.

"Shut it down, Dragon, and then heal yourself."

The Shaper is having difficulty focusing through the
pain. "Talk to me, Rush."

Rush pauses. "Talk? About what?"

"Anything… a story… I need you to talk."

Rush is vaguely puzzled by the request. It is not that
he does not understand what the Shaper wants – he knows
that the Shaper needs some sort of focal point like the
tribal hum, something steady and familiar on which to
concentrate in order to heal itself – it is just that Rush does
not know any stories. Every race, every tribe, has its tales
meant to entertain as well as instruct its children,
mythologies that bind them together. But Rush was never
told such tales as a child.

"Rush, speak to me," the Shaper pleads, its voice
growing increasingly faint.

Rush takes a deep breath and plunges into the only
story that he could possibly tell.

⚦

"Once upon a time, there was a Shaper who lived on
Earth for a number of years. The Shaper's name was… shit,
I don't know, the Shaper's name was Tamarac. Tamarac
supported itself in many trades – one of them, an artist. A
painter, in fact, and quite famous on the European conti-
nent for a while, reputed to be very talented. It had even
had some of its paintings accepted into the permanent
collection of some museum in Bern. But although it could
have supported itself on its artwork alone, Tamarac was

not satisfied just doing that, so it created other identities and worked in other fields. Interior decorating, event planning, set design for movies, things of that nature.

"Then one day, when Tamarac was expecting to come into its reproductive cycle, it tracked down another Shaper from its tribe who had the same cycle. Arrangements were made and the Shapers fulfilled their reproductive duty. When they parted again, Tamarac was carrying the embryo in its body. Shortly after that, Tamarac was discovered by the agency and taken into custody.

"The scientists were quite excited to have an impregnated Shaper in their hands and conducted a serious study of the process. They monitored that fetus every minute for the entire five months in utero and, as soon as it was born, it was taken away from its parent for further study. They were aware that a Shaper child has no physical dependency on its parent beyond the womb, and foresaw no harm in removing the child from its parent.

"What they overlooked, however, was the fact that the child, lacking the presence of any adult Shaper, would be unable to bond. For all practical purposes, the Shaper child grew up tribeless. It did not learn, as Shaper children invariably learn before the age of five, the rites and rituals of its people. It did not properly form its special Shaper senses, the ones that connect and unify the members of a tribe, that makes them instinctively seek out and protect one another. But the scientists were not aware of the damage they were causing. They raised the child amongst themselves, for their own purposes, in a sterile, controlled environment, and then they were surprised when the child could not shift when it was old enough. There had been no den parents to teach it how to shift.

"So they had to improvise. They called in a Shaper agent who had been converted to the agency's cause. The agent's name was Tao. Tao tried to communicate with the child as Shapers do, using its senses, but the child did not understand it; it had been raised speaking only the oral language of men. By this point, it was too late to teach the child how to communicate, how to think, how to be a true Shaper. Eventually, the child did learn how to shift, although the process was long and difficult. This fucked the the child up more, of course. It didn't understand why it was different from the humans who had raised it, and it could not relate to the Shaper Tao, who was supposed to be of the same species as the child, but seemed even more alien than the humans. This confusion on the part of the child led to a general distrust of both humans and Shapers.

"When the child was mature, they put it through training. The child became a most efficient assassin. For ten years, the Shaper did its job, and was then promoted to the head of the Shaper Rehabilitation Program. The Shaper was given a permanent identity, gender and Social Security number. It was a clever move on the agency's part, hiring someone who understood the nature of Shapers perfectly, but could feel no connection to them.

"For five more years, the Shaper did its job well. Then the Shaper came into its first reproductive cycle. The Shaper did not realize what was happening to it; it thought that it had contracted some rare Shaper disease and was dying. But there was a Shaper in training at the time who was affected by the event and sought out the quickening agent. This other Shaper took the child into its womb and finished its training. It was then sent out on a job and subsequently killed. When its body was retrieved by the agency, and the autopsy revealed its pregnant condition, there was an inquisition. The agency would have preferred to have kept the child and raised it in a similar manner as its fathermother. They considered it very bad judgment on the fathermother's part to have sent the pregnant Shaper out on assignment, instead of reporting it to its superiors. The interrogation was thorough, and the Shaper was tortured and repeatedly threatened with cleansing. Finally, they allowed the Shaper to return to its post in the agency. The next time that it encountered a pregnant Shaper, and there was one occasion, the Shaper immediately handed it over to its superiors and all was forgiven, if not forgotten."

Dragon's eyes are closed, its face more peaceful, while inside, it is willing itself to heal, pushing fragments of bone out to the surface of its flesh, rejoining tissue, diverting blood from the gaping hole in its chest. "What happened to Tamarac?" it asks softly.

"Dead."

Dragon sits quietly for a moment before it opens its cool gray eyes, studying the image of Rush on the screen. "Did you tell them yet, Rush?"

"Are you going to live?" Rush demands brusquely.

Dragon tries to feel around itself. "I think so."

"Good. Story time is over. Pull yourself together and get to work," Rush orders, then breaks the connection. Dragon stares at the blank screen for a long time, thinking about Rush's story, and then it reopens the lung it had closed down for repairs and nearly chokes on a torrent of blood.

♂

Five days later, the assassin locates its next target.

The Shaper spent three days in its hotel room recovering from its injury. Even now there is great discomfort when it tries to move its right arm. However, its very first Shape – the Drake one – was left-handed, so it has no difficulty using the left. On the fourth day it went out. On the fifth day, it found the Shaman.

It was just a matter of asking the right people. The ones who had met the Shaman retained a vivid memory of it, recognized the face in the photograph right away. Dragon explained that Ka'rael was a relative of his, and there had been a death in the family, and all that anyone knew was that Ka'rael was somewhere in New York. *There had been a falling out, you see...* In the end, it managed to track down a Greek woman who knew where the Shaman was living.

Dragon stands in the shadow of an alley, looking up at a window illuminated against the dark block of buildings. Dragon waits. Dragon smokes. Eventually the light blinks out but the Shaman does not leave the building. The Shaper remains cloaked in the cool darkness of the alley for quite some time before it finally makes its move.

It slips in through the front door after deactivating the lock using a trick it had learned in Stealth class. It makes its way up the stairs to the Shaman's room, snaking its hand up inside its jacket to withdraw its gun. At the door, it cocks the weapon, raising its hand up to its shoulder, ready to fire, and deactivates the apartment door silently with the skeleton pass card in its other hand before sliding the card back into a pocket. Bracing itself, it places its hand on the doorknob.

The door swings open with a sweep of light from the hall. Ka'rael, who was asleep in the bed in the middle of the room, comes awake and sees the dark figure silhouetted in the doorway. The Shaman leaps from the bed, away from the intruder.

Dragon quickly shuts the door and snaps on the wall switch, flooding the room with light, and aims its gun at the Shaman.

Dragon does not fire immediately as it has been trained to do, when it has the advantage of surprise. Instead it stares at the Shaman in disbelief. The file had warned it, in full, scientific detail, about the nature of the Shaman, but Dragon had not been adequately prepared for the hot-blooded reality of the creature before it.

The Shaman is beautiful in its androgyny, hauntingly so. Although the Shaman was often mistaken for one gender or the other, the Shaper, being of a genderless race itself, saw neither a pretty boy nor a handsome woman; it saw a perfectly balanced being. Dragon is fascinated by the sincere purity of that face, a face similar to one in a Botticelli portrait it had seen in Florence once, in another life that now seems far away. But it is not just the Shaman's face, nor its body – a puzzle of frail, strangely interlocking, angular bones – that startles the Shaper.

Ka'rael, standing close to the wall, frightened by the intruder, squints for a moment in the sudden light, half-blinded by it. Barefoot and bare-chested, it lifts a slender arm to shield its eyes while, without being aware of the action, instinctively unfolds the wings from its back.

Dragon watches those wings uncurl, spreading out slowly, almost tentatively, as if in slow motion. So prolonged is the moment, it seems as if they will stretch out forever. Quivering, the long feathers shimmer like prisms made by sunlight though clean water; long, graceful wings a pearl essence white, shooting off moonbeams. *It is,* Dragon thinks, *an angel.* The Shaper has never seen any living creature so intriguing, so *worthy* of being emulated by a Shaper, that it marvels at the sight when it should be pulling the trigger.

All of this happens in an instant. In the next instant, Ka'rael recognizes the man with the gun pointed at its chest as the one whose pain and thoughts it heard on the street five days before. It also recognizes that its life is in danger and realizes that it must fight.

Ka'rael attacks.

The Shaman's projected consciousness cannot be seen as it dives across the room and enters the Shaper's body, as its own body, now an empty, discarded shell, slumps to the ground. But Dragon feels it, like a gush of hot air washing over it briefly before its mind suddenly goes blank. Its body shudders involuntarily as the Shaman plunges in.

Ka'rael is falling. It reaches out to grab hold of anything that will stop its rapid descent but the passage is smooth and glossy black like polished obsidian. Its wings extend, catching the air, slowing the fall. It alights on a strange, shadowed field, and scans the horizon as it draws its shimmering sword. It is at this point Ka'rael realizes that this is not a human mind, and that it is uncertain about how to proceed in such unfamiliar terrain.

The field spreads out as far as the eye can see in

every direction, and in every direction the view is the same. Tall, dead, black-barked trees are scattered across the plain; their gnarled limbs contrast with the pale sky, creating lace-like patterns. Ka'rael walks towards one of these bizarre trees. As the Shaman approaches, it perceives a figure crucified to the trunk, held aloft by thick, spider-like webbing. A young face is visible through the silver filaments which bind it: a peaceful face, eyes closed as though in sleep. Ka'rael reaches out to touch the figure and, at its touch, the tree suddenly springs to life.

Screeching, the tree sways, grows larger, the tips of its branches curling like the fingers of giant hands. Ka'rael stumbles back into the field as something unforeseeable happens. The Shaper's internal landscape shifts.

The ground rolls and falls out from underneath the Shaman. It opens its wings once more but it has already become caught in the shift, tangled in thick, tar-like fibers that stretch and vibrate around it. A garbled language fills its ears, comprised of grunts and barks that it does not understand: Shaper language. It tries to break free but the upheaval surrounding it is too swift, with no escape route.

But as suddenly as the landscape started to quake, it becomes still again. Ka'rael finds itself lying on wet pavement, sticky with blood. It is not Ka'rael's blood, but the street itself which is a blood river. In the distance there are smoking bonfires and creatures howling like coyotes. The Shaman stands among the dark buildings and spies a light at the far end of the street. It heads toward the light until it arrives at a house. It opens the door and steps inside and heads to the room which is the source of the light.

A thousand candles burn along the narrow walls. At one end of the room is an altar lined with religious paraphernalia: statuettes of multi-armed goddesses and gods with jackal heads, crucifixes, bowls, bells, flowers, and incense. Below the altar is a young man spread across a mandala of sand, chained at the wrists. It is a man with light brown hair that coils outward from his head like snakes. The room is warm and throbbing like a pulse. At first, Ka'rael does not dare touch anything. There is something beautiful and sacred about this place that Ka'rael does not wish to disturb. Yet it knows that it must do something to incapacitate the enemy if it wants to live, and it also knows that it is close enough to the core to inflict some damage. Ka'rael reaches inside its own chest and pulls out a handful of a substance like gold dust, and then it blows the dust from its hand, covering the room and everything in it.

As Ka'rael releases the last of its breath, the landscape begins to shift again. Ka'rael takes flight, soaring upwards, dodging mountains as they jut up in its path, the buildings melting into purple lakes, storm clouds forming, the air suddenly turning cold, the blood on Ka'rael's wings icing over, making flight difficult. As gravity pulls it down, it wills its own heat out to the tips of its wings to melt the ice. Soaring upwards again, it finds the obsidian passage that is growing colder, tighter, a giant esophagus trying to swallow the Shaman back down, and then Ka'rael finally breaks free of the Shaper's mind and finds itself back in its own body, staring with its own eyes at the Shaper before it.

Maybe an hour has passed, maybe only a moment. But the seed has taken root inside the Shaper. The gun quivers and then drops from the assassin's hand as it overwhelmed by a torrent of emotion, a sadness so unbearable that it causes the Shaper to fall to its knees, aching, sobbing uncontrollably, wanting to die. Ka'rael then moves to the window, knowing that the effects of the emotion that it planted are only temporary, and it must hurry. Ka'rael opens the window and climbs onto the sill and then, spreading its wings, it falls through the open window and onto the wind.

♂

Dragon sits in Rush's office, studying the ends of its long, dark hair as if searching for split ends. Rush drums his fingers impatiently on the desk. Dragon has just informed Rush that the Shaman had eluded it and debriefed him on the circumstances around its escape.

"Stop doing that," Rush snaps.

Dragon lets the strand of hair slip from its fingers and glances at Rush. "Now what do you want me to do?"

"Now you wait."

"Do you want me to wait here?" Dragon asks, curbing its contempt at the idea of remaining in the confines of the agency once more.

Rush crosses his arms over his chest. "Do you have a problem with that?"

Dragon stares at Rush, an unusual expression darkening its eyes.

"Why are you looking at me like that?" Rush snaps.

"I can sense it," Dragon says mysteriously.

"Sense what?"

"The child. It's talking. Can't you hear it, Rush?"

Rush stares at Dragon coolly. "I don't know what you're talking about," he finally says. "Maybe that Shaman gave your brains a good twirl while it was in there."

"Did you tell them yet?"

Rush breaks his gaze with the Shaper. "On second thought, I don't see any reason for you to hang around here. Consider yourself on vacation until I can track down the Shaman again."

"I'm free to go?"

"As free as you can be," Rush says. "Now, get out of here. I'll be in touch."

♂

Jeremy Butkins pours a little more wine into the saucepan as the steam warms up the kitchen. "You can never have too much wine in the sauce," he tells Kincaid O'Bryan, who sits at the kitchen table, smoking Old Gold cigarettes.

Pride has just entered the kitchen to retrieve a Diet Pepsi from the refrigerator and eyes Jeremy as he pops the cap off the bottle. "I always wondered what porn stars do in their spare time."

"I used to work in a restaurant," Jeremy explains. "But, as you can imagine, the pay wasn't quite as good as my current profession."

Pride smirks at him. "I'd rather not imagine, *domo arigato,*" he says with sarcasm and glides back out of the kitchen.

Jeremy glances at Kincaid, one of his dark eyebrows cocked. "Is he always such an asshole?"

"Oh, *hai.* Nobody does a better asshole than Max."

"Hmm… that reminds me of a line from one of my movies," he says pensively. "Hey, it's getting hot in here with all the burners going. 'Caid, do me a favor and open the door."

"Sure." Kincaid rises from his seat to unlock the sliding glass door and open it wide, letting a cool night breeze into the room. "Is there anything else you want me to do?"

"Yeah, I forgot to bring the wine out to the table. Could you?"

"Where is it?"

"I put it in the fridge to chill a bit. And tell the others that the food will be ready in a minute."

"*Kinishinai,*" Kincaid says, and takes the bottle of wine into the dining room.

Jeremy checks all his pots and pans one more time. Everything has been cooked to perfection. He empties the pasta into the strainer in the sink, shakes it, then returns the pasta to the pot. He touches the wooden sauce spoon to his lips but he is not satisfied. "Now, what did I do with that basil?" he murmurs to himself, turning around to search the counter for the misplaced spice.

He sees a strange figure standing in the patio door and he jumps back startled.

"Jesus, you scared me," he says.

"*Suimasen,*" says the girl.

He drops the spoon into the sink, spattering sauce against the white ceramic, its color vivid as fresh blood.

"Now, who the hell are you?"

She steps lightly into the kitchen, staring at Jeremy in such a way that he feels like she's photographing him with her eyes. "I'm a friend of Max Pride's."

"Oh, a *friend*."

The girl ignores his insinuating tone. "Is he here?"

"Yeah, sure. I'm making dinner for him and his wife and Kincaid."

At that moment, as if the mention of his name were a magical summoning, Kincaid returns to the kitchen. "I thought I heard…" he begins to say, but, at the sight of the intruder, his voice dies away. He blinks twice, uncertain whether he should trust his own eyes. "Dahlia!" he says. "What are you doing here? I mean, what the hell happened to you? I mean, Max is going to kill you, the film…"

"I know," says the Shaper.

"Come on, you have to tell me!"

"That depends."

"Depends on what?"

"I need to know something," the Shaper says. "Kin-caid, the information for the film about the Shapers, where'd you get it? Did you really get it from *AFAR*?"

Kincaid hesitates, shifting his weight from one leg to the other. "I can't tell you that, Dahlia."

The Shaper remains impossibly still for a moment, deep in thought. "*Sōka*," it says finally. "I want to show you something, Kincaid, and then I want you to tell me if you can actually help me or not."

"Show me what?"

"Watch closely." Dahlia holds up both of its small, pale hands before it. It closes its eyes and starts to hum. Kincaid watches as one hand shifts, elongating, stretching, changing. After a few moments, the Shaper opens its eyes and then presses its palms together, one small female hand against a much larger male hand.

"Jesus fucking Christ," Kincaid says.

Jeremy cocks the other eyebrow. "Baby, you ought to be in show business."

PART 4
THOMAS ECHO

The figure stands at the edge of the shadow, looking out of the warehouse window. The familiar figure, the familiar window, the familiar street below. It burns down the familiar cigarette. However, there is one thing which changes this scene. This time, the Shaper is not alone in the warehouse. There are five eyes upon it: Max Pride's, Kincaid O'Bryan's, and one other singular red eye which glows between the men like the end of the Shaper's cigarette. An eye that sees all and records it.

The Shaper talks. It talks about Rush. It talks about its training and the subsequent assassinations. Every so often, Pride interrupts the monologue and steers it in a more dramatic direction.

The Shaper stops speaking, staring hard out the window.

"What are you looking for?" Pride asks.

"I'm waiting for someone," admits the Shaper.

"Who are you waiting for?"

"A boy," says the Shaper. "A boy named Thomas Echo."

"Why?"

The Shaper sighs in a wistful manner. "I think I'm in love with him."

Pride does not argue with this statement as the Shaper would expect. Instead, he says, "What makes you think that?"

"Are you in love with anyone, Max?"

"You mean other than my wife?" Pride says and laughs. The Shaper doesn't respond. *So much for a sense of humor,* Pride thinks. "Yeah, I'm most deeply in love with my wife."

"Then I don't need to answer that question."

There is silence for a moment, and Pride accepts a cigarette from Kincaid and the men light up. "Could you have just as easily fallen in love with a woman, do you suppose?"

The Shaper considers this as it continues to stare out of the window. "It's possible."

"Have you ever been in love before?"

"No," the Shaper says. "I never felt anything before."

"Nothing at all?"

"Nothing at all," echoes the Shaper, and then it sees him, Thomas Echo, coming down the deserted street on his way home. It freezes in mid-movement with the cigarette poised, arm half-bent at its side, eyes sliding like hot grease from one end of the street to the other as Thomas Echo passes. It is as though an electric spark has struck the Shaper in the chest, making its heart race and setting its nerves on fire. It forgets about the men in the room, it forgets about the camera, it forgets about the Dahlia shape that it's wearing as the skin below its right eye begins to twitch. The expression on the Shaper's face changes, melting from indifference into something completely unexpected. Pride and Kincaid both recognize the look for what it is: the look of someone desperately in love. Thomas Echo disappears from view and the Shaper turns away from the window, towards the camera.

Pride takes a long drag off his cigarette. "How could it have happened?" he asks.

The Shaper stares at the camera for a long moment, clenching its jaw, deep in thought. The sounds of the city seem distant, the city is dreaming. The Shaper does not hear these dreams, only the rush of its blood and its thoughts through its very heavy head, and it unclenches its jaw.

"I don't know," it says.

☿

Dahlia tips back the beer bottle, scanning the club, savoring the last swallow of the microbrew. It sits alone at a table constructed of neon tubing near the back. It is a new venue, erected while Dahlia was imprisoned by Rush. All glass and flashing lights, the club is packed with people from various seedy subcultures, who look even sicker and paler from the neon light reflected up into their wan faces. Dahlia likes it. The name of the club, plagiarized directly from a book by William Gibson, is Dog Solitude.

Dahlia is not alone for long. A big man with a beard, who looks like he'd be more at home in a tractor-pull contest in Idaho than here, sits down without being invited, smiling at it in an unusually friendly way. "Hi, how're you doing?" he says.

"All right."

"Are you looking?"

The Shaper eyes him skeptically. "You don't look like the type who'd be selling anything, if you'll pardon my saying so."

The man keeps smiling. "You'd be surprised how often I hear that. At least it keeps me out of trouble with the law, you know, a face like this."

"I don't think I need anything," the Shaper says.

"Are you sure? I've got Ecstasy, Euphoria, LSD, mescaline, MDA, MDMA, and Hammer."

"Hammer?"

"I can give you a good deal," the tractor man is saying, but already a crumpled bill has been slipped into his hand and the transaction is over. "Have a nice day," he says, and disappears back into the crowd.

Dahlia slides the packet into a pocket. It contemplates using the drug but decides to wait. After all, it has to wake up early in order to work for Pride tomorrow, as a part of the deal they made, to untangle the graphic snarl of computer code on the special effects track. The Shaper rises from the table, slipping into its slim-cut leather jacket and black gloves.

It heads towards Pioneer Square to catch the city tram, locally referred to as the Max. It stands on the empty sidewalk, waiting for the tram, not bothering to check the schedule, figuring that the tram will come when it comes, and checking the time table wouldn't make it come any faster.

As the rumble of the Max reaches the Shaper's ears, a man steps around the corner and leans on a bench a few feet away. They board the same compartment, each taking a seat at either end. There is no one else on the tram except for an elderly woman and her dog. It is a scrawny kind of yip dog, smaller than the average house cat. It starts growling at the man. The man looks at the dog, then at its owner, and smiles coldly. "That has got to be the ugliest dog I have ever seen," he says.

The old woman stares with an open-mouth kind of horror, as though she were truly unaware that her dog were indeed ugly. Dahlia also stares at the man who was so randomly and brutally honest. He is a vaguely Nordic sort of handsome, dressed completely in black like Dahlia itself, with a long, wool overcoat and thick-soled, laced-up boots. There is a subtle androgyny to his fine features, the straw-colored hair drawn back in a tortoiseshell clip and spilling down his spine, skin pale against the dark collar of his turtleneck. He glances at Dahlia. "Isn't that the ugliest dog that you have ever seen?"

Dahlia shrugs.

The man looks at the Shaper for another moment and then turns his pale face towards the window, watching the reflection of the inside of the compartment as it shifts with the passing lights outside.

The Max comes to a halt and the Shaper exits, followed by the man in black. Slightly suspicious, Dahlia increases its pace until there is some distance between it and the man. It is not in the mood for any kind of confrontation.

The Shaper enters its building, climbs the stairs to

the third floor, and pulls out its pass key before the door. It hears footsteps below, ascending the staircase. Peering down over the banister, the Shaper releases the safety catch of the gun in its pocket, and waits.

The blond man appears on the floor below, and looks up with bright blue eyes at the Shaper above. "Hey, you know what?" he says, a taunt.

Dahlia grimaces. "What?"

"I've been reading this book, well, it's a romance novel, actually, but what I just can't understand is how people can be madly in love one minute but then break up with their loved one in the next. Does this make any sense to you? Saying one thing and then immediately doing the opposite, I mean."

The Shaper relaxes its grip on the gun in its pocket. "Blake, is that you?"

The man smiles knowingly. "Only if you're my Dragon Cello," it says, voice slipping into a more familiar cadence. "Though I've never seen you shaped like a female before. It's kind of freaky weird, frankly."

"Blake, what the hell are you doing, creeping around and following me?"

Blake shrugs its wide shoulders. "Just doing my job," it says.

Dahlia sets down two dusty wine goblets on the coffee table in the candle-lit room as Blake twists the corkscrew with the strong, nimble fingers of its male hands. What Blake says causes its kin to fumble.

"Rush sent me," it says.

Dahlia stares blankly at Blake. "To do what?"

Blake pours the wine and sets the bottle down upon the glass table with a gentle *clink*. "To find out what you're doing back in Portland, all things considered."

"I suppose you were briefed about the 'all things considered'?" Dahlia asks. Blake nods. "Well. I was under contract with Lion Productions, you know."

Blake waves a hand at it. "I don't care what you're doing. You don't have to make up something on my account. Except, of course, I will have to report something back to Rush." Blake reaches into its pocket and withdraws a notepad and pen, and scribbles something. "You can tell me the truth, Dragon. You do trust me, don't you?"

Dahlia accepts Blake's note and reads it. *This conversation is being recorded: CAREFUL*, it says. As if to prove the veracity of its words, Blake lifts the lapel of its black jacket where a nearly invisible recording device blends into the fabric. Dahlia recognizes the nature of the hardware, half-relieved that it is audio only. Dahlia gestures for the pen. "Of course I trust you, Blake. If I couldn't trust you, who could I trust?"

"Nobody."

"The truth is that I had no where else to go." Dahlia sits down, hands the paper back to Blake. "I wanted to fin-ish Pride's film. And it's not like I had another identity to go back to."

Blake reads the note which says: *Are you with me all the way?* It sets the note down on the coffee table and asks, "What did you tell Pride about your disappearance?"

"Well, I just made up a little story about how a jeal-ous ex-boyfriend of mine broke into the studio and then carried me off to the middle-of-nowhere for a few weeks until he got what he wanted. And that I eventually man-aged to get away from him."

"In other words, you basically told the truth," Blake says with a hint of irony in its thin, yet lyrical, voice. "Go on, I'm with you," it says, giving its companion a pro-foundly significant look.

Dahlia picks up the pen again, writing quickly as it speaks. "Pride was quite surprised, of course, but he seemed to find the story credible."

Blake takes the note which simply says, *Rush is one of us.* It stares at the note for a moment, then shakes its head in disbelief. Dahlia nods, takes back the note and adds another brief statement. *Rush is carrying my child.*

Blake stares at Dahlia, then makes a gesture over its stomach, far out from its body. Dahlia shakes its head, places its hand flat against its abdomen, then shrugs.

"Hmm... this is good wine," Blake remarks, although it hasn't yet touched its glass. "What is it?"

"A Californian Merlot," comes Dahlia's smooth reply.

"So tell me – did any of the Pride people say anything about Rush? Or about Lights in Space?"

"Not to me."

"Did *you* say anything about Rush?"

"I don't want to talk about Rush," Dahlia is saying as it writes. "Do you know what my first job was?"

"No, what? Lorenzo didn't tell me."

"Maybe because it *was* Lorenzo. I had to ice him."

"Lorenzo's dead?" Blake asks, seeming truly surprised.

"You didn't know?"

"Rush didn't mention it." Blake scans the note which Dahlia hands to it and then nods in agreement. Dahlia gestures for the paper and continues to write. "You know, I really liked Lorenzo. He grows on you. Kinda like mold, but still..."

"Yeah, I know. I didn't want to do it."

"It's not like you had any choice, is it?"

Dahlia hands Blake the note one final time, saying, "What about you, Blake, what have you been up to?"

Blake nods once more after it reads what Dahlia has written. It then dangles the inked page over the candle flame, watching all evidence of the scheme burn to ash. "What have I been doing?" Blake repeats as the ashes fall away from its fingers. "Why, I went to the *AFAR* headquarters in London and assassinated Calvin Pope."

"Are you sure you can keep that camera steady?"

Kincaid O'Bryan drops the lens from his eye, leaning

closer, and shouts over the music vibrating through the intricate sound system wired through the walls, floor and ceiling of Dog Solitude. "What?"

"Haven't you had enough to drink?" the Shaper yells.

Kincaid raises a drooping eyebrow, a habit he has recently picked up from the porn star. "There is no such thing."

The Shaper hasn't heard him. "What?"

Kincaid leans even closer, his nose in the Shaper's pale hair. "I said... oh, never mind."

Dahlia leans back, observing Kincaid who is all slack mouth, bleary eyes, limp fingers and radiating alcohol from his very pores, and wonders if it has made a mistake by taking him into its confidence. Kincaid notices the Shaper watching him and wonders what it would be like to have a sexual tryst with it, if it could shift in the middle of the act, if it could become a copy of Marilyn Monroe. *Shapers, the ultimate fantasy machine,* he thinks.

"Stop that," the Shaper snaps at him, as though reading his thoughts.

Kincaid protests. "I wasn't doing anything."

"Yeah, right," the Shaper says. The volume of the music drops slightly as the song changes. "Now. Film me." It waits until Kincaid returns the humming machine to his eye, then announces, "Calvin Pope is dead."

"What? When did that happen?"

"About five days ago."

"That can't be true," Kincaid denies with the fervor of a politician caught in a sex scandal. "It would have been on the news if Calvin Pope died."

The Shaper leans closer to the camera. "I'm telling you. Blake said that it killed Calvin Pope about five days ago. Another Shaper has taken his place at the *AFAR* headquarters in London. Something's going on and the agency's behind it."

"But, why?"

"Now that they've infiltrated *AFAR*, they won't have to look for us anymore, *we* will go to them." The Shaper pauses to tip back the beer bottle. "Think about it – they'd have the potential to recruit an entire army of shape-shifting assassins."

Kincaid frowns. "That can't be possible."

"Kincaid, you're in the film industry. You should know by now that *anything* is possible."

"Well, how do you know that Blake isn't lying?"

The Shaper considers this. "I don't know."

"What if Blake turns you in, rats on you?"

"Then we all end up dead: me, you, Max, Ophelia, and that porn star."

Kincaid drops the camera. *"Kichigai,"* he mutters.

"What?"

"I said you're fucking crazy!" He snaps the camera shut and shoves it into his pocket. "I need another drink."

"Kuso, you don't."

He stands. "Like hell I don't," he growls and heads for the bar.

Dahlia leans back with a cigarette, feeling the vibrations from the bass throbbing up and down its spine, concentrated in the back of its skull. It feels a migraine coming on, aggravated by the noise and stress. It is thinking about its unborn child, and it is thinking about the Shaman's escape. Dahlia thinks a lot about the Shaman: its hauntingly beautiful face, its gilded wings, its jigsaw-puzzle bones, reminding Dahlia of a sculpture it had once seen atop of a cathedral in France. Unless the Shaman continues to elude the agency, Dahlia knows that it will kill Ka'rael if it has to, just to keep Rush from giving the dreaded order of torture or cleansing. Conflicting with the desire to please Rush is another that the Shaper has: the desire to lay its eyes upon the Shaman again, to study it and take its shape. It has even dreamed about becoming the Shaman, forming its flesh into weightless feathers and taking flight. Would it be possible for it to fly?

These thoughts are soon vanquished by the Shaper's realization that tonight is a Wednesday night.

What causes the Shaper to realize that it is Wednesday is the appearance of Thomas Echo at such an early hour. As the Shaper stares, Thomas Echo meets its eye from across the club. There is a moment of tension as sharp as a razor blade inside the Shaper as they look at each other, a tension that builds with every step that Thomas takes towards the table.

The Shaper can only sit there mutely, looking up at Thomas Echo, at the harsh glare of neon light shining up into the boy's face, at the red backlight which tints the edges of that coiling snake-like hair the color of blood, at the dim, tight mouth. So it is Thomas, then, who speaks first.

"*Ne*, Dahlia, how's it going?"

"Not bad, and you?"

Thomas shrugs, keeping his hands buried in the pockets of his trench coat, tossing a strand of hair out of his eyes with a shake of his head. The Shaper studies him, looking for traces of the pain and hatred it had seen in those sensitive blue eyes the last time they met, but of course there are none, Thomas being unaware that the woman before him is the same man who betrayed him with his lover Asia.

"What have you been up to?" he asks.

"Working on this film in town."

"*Sōka...*" He glances around the club as though he were already bored with the conversation. Dahlia's heart starts to sink in its chest. "Where at?"

"Lion Productions," the Shaper replies, its mind loping along, trying to find some excuse to keep Thomas from slipping away now as he has always seemed to slip away from it in the past. As it is suffering in this manner, Kincaid returns to the table with a fresh drink.

The men exchange narrowed glances, then Thomas returns his attention to the Shaper. "Lion Productions? That's real close to where I live now. You should stop by sometime."

Dahlia's heart leaps. "When are you going to be around?"

Thomas shrugs, eyeing Kincaid up and down as if he were a suit that Thomas was going to try on for size. "I work every night except Wednesday. Should I give you my address?"

"*Hai,*" Dahlia says, groping for a pen, finding one in an inner pocket, handing it over. It watches Thomas bend over the table to imprint his scrawl on a napkin. He hands Dahlia the pen and the address and then his slender hands disappear into the deep pockets of his trenchcoat again.

"Next Wednesday, then?" the Shaper proposes as casually as it can.

Thomas shrugs again and the Shaper starts losing its nerve, its hands clutching the napkin tightly, almost tearing it. It feels Kincaid place his hand on the right side of its face but it does not register the reason behind Kincaid's intrusive touch.

"*Hai,* you can stop by," Thomas says. "I might be around."

"Sure."

"See you later," Thomas says and vanishes into the crowd.

Kincaid lifts his hand from Dahlia's face and looks at the nervous skin twitching below. "Jesus, hold yourself together, will you?" Kincaid says, and the Shaper finds that quite ironic but doesn't say so.

Rush gasps as he jolts awake in his bed in the middle of the night. He sits up, scrambling to tear the sheets off his body which is burning hot. He thought that the sheets were hands trying to smother him.

In the dream, Rush was in his natural shape. He was trapped at the bottom of a deep ravine, struggling to get out, yet every time he tried to scale either side of the ravine, loose clumps of earth would break off in his hands and he would slide back down to the bottom. Then *they* came from both sides, and Rush became more desperate to escape from the dry riverbed. He heard a voice above and saw Tao at the top of the ravine's edge, holding out its hand to help Rush. As he reached out to Tao, *they* reached out for Rush, tearing him away, pulling him down to the ground, so many hands upon him that all their faces were blotted out. Hands covered Rush's mouth, hands held down his limbs, all sound muffled by the hands on his ears, Rush howling in some ancient tongue, some dream tongue, as hands pushed inside Rush's belly and the child was torn from his womb, and then–

He wakes with the vividly sharp image lingering and his heart pounding with fear. Without thinking, Rush covers his belly with his hand in a protective manner, trying to catch his breath. There is movement below his hand, the child stirring within.

"Goddamn dreams," he whispers into the stillness around him. "Nothing to fear."

Maybe the child responds. Rush cannot hear it.

He slides out of bed and goes to the kitchen to fetch a glass of water and carries it back to the bedroom. He sits down and turns on CNN. Light from the screen bounces off Rush's dark eyes as he stares intensely at the news. On the screen, bombs are exploding in Dublin, corpses crushed under blood-spattered rubble, a heightened level of tension and violence in the renewed war. A certain Shaper instinct is talking to Rush. Rush knows that the Shaman is attracted to different kinds of places: either places of great spirituality, or places where there is massive devastation to the collective human psyche, such as a plague or war zone. Rush's instinct tells him that Ka'rael is in Dublin. He switches off CNN and places a call to Portland, Oregon.

A perpetual drizzle made Dublin colder and sadder than a lonely old widow.

"You sure picked a rotten time to be a tourist," says

the woman on the next barstool over.

Ka'rael, with its tattered cloak and a dusty knapsack at its feet, is aware that it must appear quite the vagabond.

"Where're you from?" she asks.

"New York," it says.

"Talk about out of the frying pan and into the fire. Or into the line of fire, I should say. Dangerous in these parts these days. Lots of bombs."

Ka'rael likes the way that the words flow out of her mouth, the sound of the Irish brogue. "I'm not afraid of bombs."

"I'm not afraid of bombs, either," she says, tossing a strand of red hair from her pale blue eyes. "It's the men who use them that worry me." She withdraws a pack of cigarettes and offers the Shaman one, which it declines. "I'm Keenan."

"Ka'rael," it says, shaking the hand which was offered.

"Your family Irish?"

"No."

"Ka'rael – not an old Irish name or summat?"

"Not that I know of."

Keenan continues to converse with the Shaman while it sips its lukewarm tea. It senses a freedom of spirit and a strong independence in her. Humans like this are rare. So much grief and suffering here, and, by chance cir-cumstance, it has stumbled across a brilliant soul, a flame burning brightly amidst a city of destruction.

"You traveling alone?" Keenan asks, lighting another cigarette.

"I always travel alone."

"No girlfriend back home?"

Ka'rael smiles his golden smile. "To tell you the truth, I'm not really into that sort of thing."

"Oh," she says. "The sex thing or the woman thing?"

"Well, neither."

"No!" she says. "Are you slagging me?"

"Am I – what?"

"Joking," she says. "You're a virgin then. Usually I can tell a virgin when I see one." She glances up as the door of the pub opens. "Now, that beautiful man that just walked in is obviously not a virgin."

Ka'rael glances at the tall man in the faded denim jacket who is approaching the bar. He has a young face, a dark ponytail, and, yes, he is truly beautiful. Maybe the most beautiful man Ka'rael has ever seen. His lyrical, Irish-accented voice floats over the bar as he speaks to the bar-maid. "Pint of plain, love," he says. He turns and smiles at Keenan. "Howya, miss," he says.

"Hello," she says. "Fancy meeting you here."

"Small world, innit?" he says and takes his drink in hand. "I've feckin' run out of fags. You got one, love?"

Keenan hands him a cigarette. He glances at Ka'rael and their eyes meet: burnt sienna brown and Chinese porcelain green.

"You're a stranger to Dublin, aren't you?" he says. "If you don't have a place to stay, I can highly recommend one to you. This lass's ma runs a nice bed and breakfast outside the city. The breakfast is brilliant."

"I do need a place to stay, so thank you," says Ka'rael.

"I would've mentioned it," she admits. "Although a recommendation from an actual guest is more convincing than a sales pitch from the owner's daughter."

"It's quite lovely," says the man. "I'd give it four stars. Or should that be five? Well, whatever, the point is that it's bloody grand. I'd be happy to show you the way. Once you finish your tea, of course."

"It sounds perfect," Ka'rael says. "Why not?"

As night falls outside the guesthouse, Ka'rael stretches its legs out in front of the fireplace, looking at the beautiful Irish boy in the armchair across from it who asks, "You sure I can't offer you a drop of whiskey?"

"I don't drink alcohol," Ka'rael says.

"That's probably for the best. I have a friend who's obviously drinking himself to death. A terrible thing to watch. I wish I could just get inside him, fix what's wrong…"

A small smile creeps across Ka'rael's mouth.

"I've seen too many terrible things," the man says softly. "Sometimes… sometimes I feel like I've had enough of this world."

"What do you mean?" Ka'rael asks, not liking this turn in the conversation, suspecting that this young man might be on the verge of suicide. Not what he would have expected, given the cheerful quality of the light banter they'd shared for the past hour. *I could go in,* Ka'rael thinks, *but, no, not yet. Wait.*

"I think you know what I mean, Ka'rael."

The Shaman pauses, staring at the beautiful dark eyes, the beautiful dark mouth, and the beautiful dark hair framing the perfect face in soft wisps, freed from its elastic band. The Shaman, like all of its people, puts a great value on objects of beauty, maybe the reason why it agreed to come to this stranger's room. But now it feels uneasy. The Shaman tries to pick up on any emotion that the boy may be projecting, but there is none. None at all. Which makes the Shaman even more uneasy.

"How do you know my name?" it asks. "I never told you."

"Keenan told me."

The Shaman narrows its eyes. "Are you… are you lying to me?"

The beautiful boy slowly leans forward in his chair. He speaks clearly, in a completely different tone of voice, a voice with an American accent, the Irish brogue having disappeared without a trace. "I'm going to tell you a few things and then I want you to tell me if you can help me or not."

"Who are you?"

"I'm called Dragon Cello. I work for Rush. Do you know who I'm talking about?"

"The one with the dancing soul," Ka'rael says. "I met another one like him in New York... That was you, wasn't it?"

The Shaper nods, staring at the Shaman with unblinking eyes.

Fear and disgust for the creature before it chills the Shaman's blood. "You're an assassin!" it cries. With an amazing agility, it leaps from the chair.

Dragon also leaps from its chair. The tumbler of whiskey falls from its lean hand and shatters on the floor. Dragon is on top of the Shaman before the Shaman is even aware that the Shaper moved, and it is shocked to find itself in the assassin's arms. Before Ka'rael can react, Dragon forces the Shaman down below its bigger, stronger, male body, pinning its wrists to the bed.

"Listen to me!" Dragon says. "I'm not going to kill you. If I wanted to kill you, I could have done it already!"

The Shaman feels the desperation behind the Shaper's plea, almost tangible, a pulse of emotion coursing down an invisible thread between them, intensified by the physical contact. Quitting its struggle, it looks up into the Shaper's face above it, seeking, seeking, then asks, "Why didn't you?"

Something flickers briefly in Dragon's eyes as it loosens its grip on Ka'rael's wrists. "When I saw you that first time in New York, in the moonlight..."

"What?"

Dragon stares down at those pale limbs, the long throat, the jade eyes, the androgynous face. "I thought that you were the most beautiful thing I'd ever seen," it blurts out. "Like an angel."

Ka'rael turns its face away. "Don't say that."

Dragon realizes after a moment that the Shaman is crying. "What's wrong? I told you that I'm not going to hurt you."

"I'm not beautiful."

"Yes, you are," Dragon insists. "You're even more beautiful when you're crying like that, but I wish you'd stop." The Shaper reaches for the cord that fastens the Shaman's cloak, untying the knot. It smooths the cloak back from the Shaman's shoulders and then takes the Shaman's face in its hands, gently wiping the tears from its skin. "Since I saw you in New York, I haven't been able to stop thinking about you. You're fascinating."

Misty-eyed, Ka'rael remains motionless as the Shaper touches it. Long fingers trail along the Shaman's bones, stroke its neck, filter through its hair. Given the situation – Ka'rael lying below the Shaper on the bed – and the way the Shaper's dark eyes smolder, it makes an assumption. "A seduction is pointless," Ka'rael says. "You can't make love to me. This body isn't made that way."

Something else flickers through the Shaper's eyes, some chord has been struck, some painful memory. The Shaper withdraws from the Shaman on the bed and moves toward the fireplace.

"Neither is mine, really. Not in my true form. What we do, I wouldn't call it making love. We reproduce once every five years but I don't know what it felt like because I don't remember." Dragon grimaces. "Not that I really want to remember."

The Shaman sits up. "Why not?"

"Because of who it was with," Dragon says. Then it laughs, a hollow sound. "Mister dancing soul himself."

"This – it makes you suffer, doesn't it?"

The Shaper shrugs. "There's nothing I can do about it. It doesn't matter." It watches the crackling flames in the hearth for a moment, then turns back to the Shaman, recalling something it has read in the Shaman's file. "Your kind – you're intimate, or whatever you want to call it, using your minds, right?" The Shaman nods. "And you – you were in my head."

"I... yes, I was."

"Is it a good place or a bad place?"

The Shaman smiles kindly. "It intrigued me." It folds its hands in its lap, casting its eyes down. "Actually, if you're willing... I would like to enter your mind again."

The Shaper cocks one eyebrow, then puts on a wry smile. "To be honest, I wasn't too crazy about what you did to me last time."

"I only hurt you because I thought I had to," Ka'rael says. "I promise it wouldn't happen again."

The Shaper considers this. "All right. What do you want me to do?"

The Shaman pulls the large t-shirt up and over its head, freeing its wings, letting them uncurl and fully extend. Dragon stares in awe, as before. The Shaman kicks off its boots and reaches for the buckle on its belt, giving Dragon a *What are you waiting for?* look. "Well? Take off your clothes."

Surprise causes Dragon to fumble. "I, uh, thought this wasn't a seduction."

"It's easier if there's physical contact," says the Shaman.

⚥

Dragon wakes in the arms of the Shaman. Wings all around it, a comforter made of warm, breathable down. Never has the Shaper felt as safe as this, as warm, or so full of heady optimism. Dragon opens its eyes and sees silver-sheened gold, the morning sunlight filtering through the translucent tips of those spectacular, unearthly wings. It looks at the Shaman's peaceful face resting against the Shaper's broad shoulder. The Shaman then shifts in the bed, opens its eyes, and looks at the Shaper.

Dragon smiles. Ka'rael recognizes the smile to be genuine and not a Shaper affectation. Ka'rael knows a lot more about the Shaper's internal landscape than anyone else in the universe, and it knows that it possesses more brightness than darkness; it sees great beauty in the continuous shifting of the landscape within. Ka'rael, being of the race that it is, has a great capacity for love. Ka'rael is in love with the Shaper's mind, which is, for the Shaman, the only true way to be in love. For this reason it says, "What can I do to help you?"

Dragon reaches out and strokes the Shaman's bare shoulder with a slow and deliberate gesture. The Shaper is thinking. What is the Shaper thinking on this morning, in this warm and safe room full of peace and love, immersed in the serenity of the Shaman's presence, as they clasp each other like two lovers who have found each other after a long and painful absence, while outside bombs are falling, blood is spilling, anger hot and turbulent like a storm bursting, the stench of death permeating every nook and alley of the war-damaged city? Is it thinking about Rush or the child or Blake or the movie or its crew or the gentle touch of the beautiful Shaman? Actually, it is not. It is touching the warm skin of the Shaman in its arms, but it is thinking about Thomas Echo. Today is Tuesday. Tomorrow is Wednesday, when Thomas "might be around" his apartment. And Dragon is here, so far away from the man it loves, in Ireland.

"Go to Portland," says the Shaper.

⚥

Wednesday night in Portland. Interior hall. Kincaid O'Bryan stands before an apartment door. His pulse is sluggish from all the tequila he'd slugged back earlier at Dog Solitude. His head is a little numb, his hands cold. He blinks a few times and then presses the doorbell.

The door swings open to reveal a young, unfamiliar face.

"Hi," says Kincaid, "I'm looking for... umm... Dahlia."

The ethereal green eyes stare at him with a recognition that Kincaid finds a little strange because he is certain (well, fairly certain, since his memory sometimes plays tricks on him, things like misplacing his keys inside the icebox, or omitting the part where he took some girl home with him after a particularly heavy night on the bottle) that he doesn't know this boyishly slim blonde girl before him.

"I'm a friend of Dahlia's," says the Shaman. "Come in."

Shrugging, Kincaid shuffles in as Ka'rael closes the door behind him.

"So, what's your name?" Kincaid asks as he glances around the living room in a casual but curious manner. For someone who makes a living programming code, there's a conspicuous lack of technology. A moderate amount of dinged-up, secondhand furniture from a variety of decades suggests the temporary nature of its home. And, apparently, Shapers must like to read a lot because there are shelves lined with dozens of musty paperback books against the wall.

"Ka'rael," says the Shaman, sitting down beside him.

"So, is Dahlia here?"

"No, it had an appointment."

Kincaid pauses before asking, *"Suimasen,* what did you say?"

Ka'rael's consciousness is open enough to allow it access to Kincaid's surface thoughts. Not that it is very difficult, considering that the man is drunk and most of his mental barriers have thinned substantially with every drop of alcohol.

"I know about the Shaper."

"Sōka," says Kincaid, looking closely at what he thinks is a pretty young girl in front of him. "Are you a Shaper, too?"

Ka'rael smiles its kind and beautiful smile. "No, I'm not."

"Oh. Is there anything to drink around here?"

"Other than water or coffee, no," Ka'rael says. "Would you like me to make you a cup of coffee?"

Kincaid sighs and leans back against the sofa. "Eh, why the hell not?"

After waiting alone in the living room for a few minutes, Kincaid wanders into the kitchen as the stove-top espresso maker starts to gurgle throatily. He watches

Ka'rael lean over to turn off the burner: the blond hair falling down around the shoulders of its oversized and lumpy wool sweater, the twist of the slim hips below a torn pair of jeans that reveal purple tights beneath.

Looking up, Ka'rael smiles.

☿

Cut scene. Interior hall. Across town the Shaper is standing before an apartment door. Its pulse is rapid and unsteady from a bad case of nerves. Its head is tumbling with a thousand different thoughts, its hands hot. It doesn't blink as it presses the doorbell.

The door swings open to reveal a young, familiar face.

"Hi," says the Shaper.

"Hi," says Thomas. "How's it going?"

"It's going," the Shaper says and shrugs.

"You want to come in?"

"*Hai.*"

The Shaper whispers in as the boy closes the door behind it. It drops down to the sofa uninvited.

"So, what's your job like?" Thomas asks as he sits beside Dahlia.

"It's a job," says the Shaper, reaching nervously for a cigarette. "Actually, I just finished today."

"You have another film lined up?" Thomas asks, reaching forward to steal a cigarette from the pack on the table. The proximity of him causes the Shaper's hand to tremble a little. It reaches up to smooth its long, blond hair behind an ear to keep Thomas from noticing its fierce nervousness.

"Not with Lion Productions. I might have to leave town soon to find something."

"*Sōka,*" says Thomas, eyeing the Shaper up and down in a cool manner that makes the Shaper start wishing that it were a Shaman and could read emotional transmissions. "When would you leave?"

"Not sure. Is there anything around here to drink?" the Shaper asks.

"There might be some wine in the kitchen," Thomas says. "Would you like some?"

"Wine would be good," says the Shaper.

After a few minutes, Thomas returns from the kitchen with a pair of mismatched glasses and a cheap bottle of Idaho wine. The Shaper watches him as he leans over to set the glasses down on the table: the tight, tense mouth, the grace of his slim body twisting below a baggy black t-shirt bearing a ghoulish reproduction of Bela Lugosi's face.

As he pours, he meets Dahlia's eyes. He doesn't smile.

♂

Cut back to the Shaper's apartment. Ka'rael pours Kincaid another cup of coffee but the effects of the alcohol are still strong. Kincaid doesn't feel a thing except for a spark of interest in the creature sitting there talking to him about the terrible war in Dublin.

Kincaid sets down the coffee cup. "Tell me something. How do you know Dahlia, anyway? I mean, umm, you know what's going on."

Ka'rael folds its hands in its lap. "The Shaper came to New York to kill me, but it couldn't pull the trigger."

He laughs nervously."Ha, ha, you've got to be kidding me, but I wouldn't be able to pull the trigger either. Of course, I'm not a trained killer."

"No, you aren't," Ka'rael says softly.

Kincaid shifts on the sofa, looking at Ka'rael. *"Ne,* why was Dahlia trying to kill you? I mean, it was a job, right? And what are you doing here, then? The Shaper saved your life, so you owe her – or it, or whatever – you owe it something?"

"No. I came because I would do anything for the Shaper."

"Huh. Are you in love with the Shaper?"

"Oh, yes," the Shaman admits freely.

"*Nanda?* I mean, you do know that Dahlia is in love with some boy, don't you?"

Ka'rael smiles. "It doesn't matter. The love I have knows no conditions, no boundaries. It is something I give. I do not expect anything in return. There are no limitations. I give love to all those who accept it."

Kincaid leans forward, taking Ka'rael by the shoulders. When he encounters no resistance, he presses his lips against the Shaman's. The Shaman allows Kincaid to kiss it but it doesn't feel passion. It feels compassion. Kincaid mistakes this passivity for something else.

"Do you want to go to the bedroom?"

"All right," says Ka'rael.

In the Shaper's bedroom, he lays down across the unfamiliar bed.

Ka'rael climbs up beside him. "Close your eyes, Kincaid. Let yourself relax."

Kincaid smiles. "Okay," he says, and, as the Shaman lays its hands upon him, Kincaid starts to fall: away from consciousness, away from himself, into a trance.

Then Ka'rael is inside the writer's mind, seeking out the fears that lurk there. The fears are old, strong and determined, but the Shaman is older, stronger and more determined. Wings spread, the Shaman soars with the grace of an eagle through Kincaid O'Bryan's internal landscape, striking down the dark demons that thrive in a river of alcoholic desperation.

Inside, way down deep in Kincaid's subconscious, the Shaman finds a little boy huddled in a dark corner. Ka'rael recognizes the child to be Kincaid's true self which has been stunted by pain and emotional trauma. Ka'rael kneels down before the child and opens its arms in a non-threatening manner.

"Hello, there," it says, as the child looks at it with fear and wonder. "It's okay. You can come out now."

The boy hesitantly reaches out a hand toward the

golden, sexless, winged creature before it. A creature about which legends and religions are made. Ka'rael smiles beatifically as there is contact.

⚥

Thomas pours Dahlia another glass of wine and the effects of the alcohol are starting to kick in. The Shaper's emotions are on overdrive. It feels frightened, exhilarated, agitated and depressed all at once because of the boy sitting there talking to it about how life just sucks.

Dahlia sets down its empty wine glass. "Well," it says.

Thomas stares at it. "You know, I've been thinking about you a lot."

The Shaper's heart takes a bold leap into its throat like a contender for the gold medal in the high jump. "Oh? What have you been thinking?"

Thomas shrugs. The Shaper remembers how frustrating that noncommittal gesture used to be. It wonders why it has forgotten all the bad things.

"Different stuff," he says finally.

"Like what?"

Thomas stares with his half-drunk gaze directly into the eyes of the Shaper before him. "Like how you used to open your eyes while I was kissing you. Do you still do that – open your eyes when someone's kissing you?"

"I don't know," the Shaper says, "but there is one way to find out."

Thomas leans forward and kisses the Shaper, who wraps itself around him, getting lost in those familiar lips, lost in that thick, familiar snake hair. Many moments pass before Thomas pulls back. He stands up, holding out his hand. The Shaper takes it and lets Thomas lead it into the bedroom.

He lays down across the bed which should be unfamiliar to the Shaper but isn't, while the Shaper has excused itself to the bathroom.

Fingers grasping the edges of the sink, the Shaper

throws back its head with a gasp, its eyes watering as the Hammer shoots up its nasal passages and down its throat. Its heart quickens, its head throbbing, as it wipes its nose and then checks its reflection in the mirror. "Everything's okay," it whispers to its reflection. As if in reply, Dahlia hears Blake's warning voice swim through its candyfloss sticky thoughts. "It won't kill me," the Shaper whispers, trying to reassure itself. It has no real choice at the moment except to be reassured. Once the Shaper has regained its composure, it returns to the bedroom where Thomas Echo waits.

With every passing minute, the drug saturates the Shaper's bloodstream, swelling its head, causing its heart to pound faster, bringing strange and unfamiliar sensations to the surface of its skin, as an even stranger sensation intensifies at the bottom of the Shaper's gut. The sensation that the Shaper is experiencing is drug-induced ecstacy. It groans in earnest as Thomas touches it, his mouth on its throat. The Shaper is lost to its own demanding lust.

"Take me," the Shaper hisses into the boy's ear, and in response he shifts his hips and then he is inside.

The Shaper, back arching, eyes closing, hands clutching, is being hit hard by the drug and is in trauma. But the trauma is not as painful as it is pleasurable. In other words, the Shaper is having an orgasm. It marvels at the flood of ecstatic tension that is overwhelming its body, even as it dimly wonders if it is dying from whatever toxins compose the Hammer.

Then again, the Shaper's brain has been so severely affected that it does not particularly care whether it is dying or not, its thinking cloudy, distorted. In fact, when it looks up at Thomas through its half-closed eyes, it is not Thomas' face that the Shaper perceives. In the midst of its fog, it sees the face of Rush before it, an interesting subconscious trick. Yet, things are not so distorted that the Shaper does not hear and comprehend the word that slips off the boy's lips as he reaches his own climax.

The word on Thomas Echo's lips is: "Asia…"

What the Shaper perceived to be the peak of the Hammer, the sudden flux of sexual pleasure, was not the climax for the Shaper. When the drug does hit the Shaper at its true peak, it affects a different set of synapses altogether.

It strikes at the Shaper's limbic system. Suddenly the Shaper is full of fear and anger, an irrational and uncontrollable fury. It shoves the boy away from it with its shaking, shaking hands and then it loses all conscious thought as primal instinct takes over.

Ka'rael returns from the depths of Kincaid's darkness, so weary. It looks down at Kincaid, who is now sleeping off the effects of the tequila, his expression one of peace, the result of the great internal changes that Ka'rael has instigated. Feeling safe here next to Kincaid in the Shaper's bed, Ka'rael closes its eyes and immediately falls into a state similar to a deep and dreamless sleep.

--- it sees the wet road in front of it, feels the rain streaking down its face --- its face --- there's something dreadfully wrong with its face. It has a sudden moment of lucidity: *How did I get here? And Thomas? What happened to Thomas? What have I done?* People are staring at the Shaper, it lifts its hand to its face and realizes that at some point it shifted and then it feels more fear --- it doesn't remember when or where it shifted --- it doesn't recognize the clothes it's wearing --- this face feels something like the Dragon shape --- the hands look like the Dragon hands --- the hands are covered with blood --- *ohmygod what have I done?* the Shaper says or maybe it just thinks it and then the thoughts go away again ---

--- it walks on down the hall, it knows the carpeting

of this hallway --- colors fly through its head --- the crunch of shattered glass under its feet --- its feet are bare --- the walls are breathing and swaying around it --- red and warm like a mammalian birth canal --- it knows that Ka'rael is there and it thinks, half-aware, that Ka'rael will help it --- *Ka'rael so beautiful like an angel not like that Echo boy no Ka'rael like love loved would-be should-be lover manwoman brothersister soul mate* ---

--- the bedroom, there, it sees them, it sees them together in the bed --- it is overcome with a jealous rage --- a protective instinct --- it knows that the gun is in the drawer --- it knows what pulling a trigger is like --- it knows that love is beautiful and betrayal is ugly, so very, very ugly --- the Shaman opens its eyes and the Shaper can taste its fear, as strong as the bitter rage that already fills the Shaper's mouth --- and it points the gun at the Shaman and it knows better than to hesitate this time ---

♂

The Shaman comes awake in the middle of the night and sees Dragon in the dim light. It sees the Shaper's half-bare skin marred by cuts and coated with glass dust; it sees blood, although it cannot discern whether all of it belongs to the Shaper or not; it sees the eyes, not Dragon's dark brown eyes, but a pale shimmering gray color, a quicksilver pool around a pupil the size of a pinprick.

But it's not what the Shaman sees that frightens it as much as what it senses. Beams of crazy, high-intensity emotion shoot off the Shaper: jealousy, hatred, madness and rage, abnormal amounts for even the most distressed of human men; the Shaper is truly out of its mind. The Shaman, so overwhelmed by the pain of the being that it loves, is too shocked to move even as the Shaper extends its weapon toward the bed, instead staring like an animal in the middle of the highway into the headlights of a vehicle that is about to run it down.

Kincaid, when he opens his eyes in the middle of the

night, sees the demented Shaper taking a gun from the drawer by the bed and raising it, the barrel aimed at the Shaman beside him. The cock of the gun resonates in Kincaid's aching head and he realizes what is about to happen, and this sudden realization causes him to cry out.

"Jesus God, no!" he screams and then there is a single deafening explosion as the Shaper fires the gun.

Rush reaches over and presses the intercom button. "Tell me."

"Agent Dragon is here."

"Send it in," Rush orders and leans back in his chair. He is looking forward to the explanation of why Dragon returned to Portland after having been dispatched to Dublin to deal with the matter of the Shaman. There was going to be hell to pay, and if there was one thing in which Rush excelled, it was giving hell.

The door opens and the Shaper steps in. It wears a pair of Armani sunglasses and is carrying a very large and frayed burlap rice sack in one hand.

Rush stands up, resting his hands on the desk before him. "You better start talking now and it fucking better be good or I'll cleanse you myself."

Dragon tosses its beautiful hair. "Stay calm, Rush."

Rush puts on a sarcastic smile. "I'm *always* calm."

Dragon returns the smile. "Oh, yes, I forgot."

"Now enough of the pleasantries, you piece of shit Shaper. What happened to the Shaman?"

The smile slides straight off the Shaper's face like oil from water. "That's why I'm here, Rush, to tell you."

"At least you've got something right."

Dragon approaches the desk, opening the sack. "I think we have a difference in opinion about what is right and what isn't. Killing the Shaman – I don't think that I would call that right."

"What you think isn't important. Now, tell me. Is the

Shaman dead?"

"I can do better than tell you." From the sack Dragon withdraws a lump of bloodied feathers and drops it on the desk before Rush. Rush does not touch the lifeless, dull thing that lies on the desk before him, but he recognizes it, without a doubt, as the wings of the Shaman.

"Good," he says.

♂

Kincaid looks at his watch and then steps up to the payphone at the space station. Around him, rocket engines roar, making it difficult to hear the ringing of the line which he is trying to reach. He feels nervous, but also surprisingly good. He has not had a drink in three days. A voice responds to his call, a voice that he knows.

"It's going down," Kincaid says and then disconnects without another word.

♂

The intercom buzzes again.

"Agent Blake is here."

"I'm in an important meeting," Rush snaps. "Blake can wait."

There is a small hesitation. "Blake says that it's code red."

"Fine," Rush relents. "Send Blake in."

He clicks off the intercom and looks at Dragon.

Dragon leans closer to him. "Rush, would you take off your sunglasses for a moment?"

"Whatever for?"

"Just humor me, will you?" Dragon says, lifting its own shades and slipping them into a pocket. "There's something I need to tell you and I want to see your eyes when I say it."

"You're such a pain in the ass," Rush says, but he removes the sunglasses anyway and sets them down on the desk. His doe eyes meet Dragon's for a moment and Dragon opens its mouth as if to say something, but then the door swings open and Rush looks away from Dragon as Blake enters.

At this moment, with Rush's defenses down, Dragon strikes. It hits Rush in the face with its fist as hard as it can. Rush staggers backward from the force of the blow. Dragon leaps over the desk and is on top of Rush, knocking him to the ground, punching him twice more in the face, bloodying a lip and breaking his nose. Rush groans with the pain, but manages to kick Dragon's leg out from under it. Dragon stumbles but catches itself quickly on the edge of the desk. Rush tries to pull himself up off the floor but Dragon kicks him back down, Rush's head striking the ground so hard that his vision starts to swim.

Through the haze he sees Blake and Dragon now standing over him, the same unblinking eyes in different hues, the same, slick ponytails, the same dark suits. Blake withdraws a weapon from its pocket and aims it at Rush's face. Rush recognizes it immediately as a Disabler gun.

"I hate to say this," Blake says. "But, you know, I'm going to enjoy the hell out of making you suffer. This is for what you did to me, what you did to Dragon –"

"Don't forget Lorenzo," Dragon adds.

"Oh, yeah, and Lorenzo, too," Blake says, "and… oh, forget it, there's too much shit to list. Consider yourself disabled, you lying prick."

Rush closes his eyes, trying to prepare himself, but he knows that nothing can prepare him for that. Rush, like any other Shaper who has already experienced the effects of the Disabler ray, is deathly afraid. "God, no, don't," he pleads, even though he knows that it's futile to beg mercy from merciless creatures.

"Wait." Dragon places a hand on Blake's arm. Blake looks inquisitively at its cousin. "The child," Dragon explains.

Though reluctant, Blake nods and lowers the gun. It takes a syringe from its pocket and flicks off the cap. "Hold him down," Blake says, and Dragon pins Rush to the floor as Blake slides the needle in.

Almost immediately Rush feels the drug begin to work and his senses start to dim. He hears Blake say something like *Get on with it I'll get the sack*, but Rush doesn't understand, he cannot move or cry out, the drug has made him a prisoner in his own body. Dragon is humming, shifting quick as lightning striking, melting into a different shape. Rush sees himself standing above him, sees himself reaching for the sunglasses on the desk and slipping them on.

"Well, what do you think?" Dragon asks, wearing Rush's voice.

"You're so perfect, it's fucking creepy," Blake says.

Rush tries to move but he feels like he has been pumped full of lead as their hands come at him, just like in that dream, and then he realizes what Blake meant as he is thrown like a potato into the bloody burlap sack. Everything fades to black as Rush's consciousness slips away from him like an assassin slipping away in the night.

PART 5
MR. RUSH

Rush slowly drifts into consciousness. Primarily he is aware of the throb of pain in the back of his skull and the difficulty of breathing. Grunting with the effort, he reaches up to touch his face, feeling the swollen flesh of his nose and mouth. Further awareness brings the memory of how his face became so swollen and it occurs to Rush that he has no idea where he is.

He surveys his surroundings and is not terribly surprised to find himself locked in a cell, although what cell he couldn't say. As he sits up, a shock of pain rolls through his head and he suppresses the urge to be sick. A moment passes and Rush rises from the floor – there is no bed – and crosses to the bars. Looking out, he finds no clues that reveal his whereabouts, and he sees no signs of life, only a long, empty corridor.

Rush is thinking. If the Shapers had wanted to kill him, he wouldn't be here now – he knows that much. So they must have some other plan, but what? As Rush brushes the hair away from his face with both hands, the room quivers.

Rush grabs at the bars to steady himself. "What the…" he murmurs, but then realization strikes. This is no earthquake. In fact, Rush is no longer on Earth. He's been abducted and placed on a spaceship.

Rush swears softly. He feels a sudden heaviness at the pit of his stomach, which may or may not be due to the pull of artificial gravity. He calls out, his voice echoing down the empty corridor. He waits in the silence, and then calls out again.

The door at the end of the corridor slides open and Dragon Cello walks through. Dragon moves slowly towards the bars and stops a few feet in front of Rush. They stand staring at each other for a few tense moments without speaking. Then Dragon crosses its arms before its chest and says, "You don't look so good, Rush."

"I wonder why," Rush says, seething sarcasm.

"Glad to see you've retained your sense of humor," Dragon says, staring directly into Rush's eyes until Rush averts his gaze. "Feeling naked without your shades?"

Rush lifts his chin, defiant. "You and your damn attitude. I should've had you cleansed."

Dragon smiles coldly. "Maybe."

Rush grits his teeth. "Tell me where we are."

"No."

"What do you mean, 'no'?"

Dragon laughs. "Rush, you can't give orders anymore. No one's going to listen to you. You should just shut the fuck up and be grateful that you're not dead."

"Fuck you."

"Such hostility."

Rush squeezes the bars between his hands. Close together, but not too close, and, more importantly, lacking a grid to stun. "You really think I couldn't shift my way out of this cage?"

"Not without risk of damaging the child. Which is something I don't think even *you* would do."

Rush stares at it in an unblinking Shaper way.

"Besides," Dragon says airily, "orders have been given to shoot any strangers on sight. I suggest you stay in there, where it's much safer."

"You bastard."

Dragon turns to leave, but then pauses to add, "If you need anything, all you have to do is ask. You do know how to ask, don't you? You take an order and put something like 'Would you please' in front of it."

Dragon starts walking back down the corridor. Rush follows it with his eyes. "Dragon," he finally says, and the

Shaper stops. "Would you please tell me where we're going?"

Dragon considers this. "No."

Before Dragon reaches the door, Rush makes another attempt. "Well, would you please bring me a fucking aspirin or something?"

Dragon considers this as well. "Yeah, sure. I'll have someone bring you an aspirin."

The door wooshes shut.

Rush swears under his breath a few times, and leans back against the wall of his tiny and dismal cell. He reflects on what Dragon said about the child. Although it doesn't show as more than a slight roundness of the belly, he is aware of how large the child has become; he can feel the weight and heft of it, and knows it is too big to fit between the bars. Next, he contemplates his revenge. He closes his eyes, imagining various gruesome scenarios tainted with buckets of Dragon's blood, and that makes him feel better. When he hears the whisper of the door again, he opens his eyes. He recognizes the person who approaches, carrying a bottle of water in one hand and some painkiller in the other, which are handed warily to Rush through the bars.

"It's been a long time, Rush," says the familiar voice, with no trace of either animosity or sympathy. Rush swallows the pill with a swig of water, regarding his nurse with an intense look, trying to figure out just what had gone wrong. It dawns on him how all of this happened, how he ended up a prisoner of his prisoners, the victim of his victims.

Goddamned movie special effects wizard.

"I really thought that you were dead," Rush muses.

"I know," says Ka'rael.

Kincaid O'Bryan and Max Pride stand on the deck of the spaceport, each holding a camera eye in the direction of the ship as it rises into the air. Pride is wearing earplugs to block out the continual buzz of engines that swarms about them, but he cannot block the taste of dust and burning chrome that fills his mouth. Kincaid wears no such ear protection since his hearing has not yet returned to normal. Three days ago, when the Shaper shot the gun at that uncomfortable proximity, the blast caused Kincaid's ears to start ringing. Although the medics said that the damage would not be permanent, he'd suffered a slight loss of hearing. Kincaid was mostly grateful that he had not received any other damage that night.

That was something he would never forget, the moment in which he came awake and saw a stranger with the gun aimed at the Shaman. At that point, neither he nor Ka'rael had any idea how badly the Shaper was hallucinating. Kincaid cried out. The gun discharged.

The bullet flew out of the gun and blew straight through the mattress between Kincaid and Ka'rael, completely missing its target. The Shaper started to shake so violently that the gun slipped from its fingers and clattered to the floor. The Shaper fell to its knees and spoke in a shaky voice.

"Ka'rael – help me," it said.

The Shaman then slipped from the bed and took the Shaper into its arms, stroking its glossy head, and Kincaid watched this scene, blinking a few times because he thought he saw wings extending from the back of the blond who'd just been in bed with him. He knew, after all, that the light was dim and that he was still half-drunk and only half-awake and possibly in shock, but, yeah, those were wings all right.

Trembling like a frightened child, Dragon clung to the Shaman, pleading incoherently in the shadows.

"I love you," the Shaman replied, enfolding the Shaper in its wings.

Yeah. No doubt about it. Fucking *wings.*

Eventually the ship disappears from sight, and Pride and Kincaid drop the cameras from their eyes and glance at each other. Something passes between them; they know that there is nothing left to film. They had used their connections to help Dragon get on the outward bound ship, manned by a small crew and carrying less than a dozen scientists on a geological expedition, and now the story, the documentary, is finished. They look at each other with a *Now what?* expression.

Pride stuffs his camera into his pocket. "You know this will never see print," he says.

⚥

Dragon dreams. Fire-breathing, black-scaled eels swim through the air, weaving in and out of the dark and howling like mating Shapers. There is blood in the dream. There is a gun in Dragon's pale and malformed hand. From out of the darkness Thomas Echo emerges, speaking words that Dragon does not want to hear. Blood and smoke bloom on the boy's chest and the gun becomes hot in Dragon's hand and Dragon starts to shift into someone else.

Dragon wakes and jerks up in its bed. In the dim light it sees Ka'rael still sleeping soundly beside it. In sleep, Ka'rael resembles an angel even more. Dragon rises, slipping into its shirt and heading for the door. There is a soft rustling of sheets on skin as Blake rolls over in its own bed on the other side of the cabin.

Dragon goes to the canteen and selects a hot tea from the beverage dispenser, pressing the panels for lemon and sugar. As the liquid dribbles into the cup, Dragon stares off at nothing, contemplating its dream.

Dragon does not remember anything that happened from the time it left Thomas Echo's apartment to when it found itself in the Shaman's arms. They did not dare seek medical attention for the Shaper, of course. The Shaman had stayed with Dragon through the ugly twenty-four hour comedown, tending its wounds, applying cold compresses, and speaking words of comfort, having sent Kincaid away to the hospital.

Dragon thinks about the hospital as it picks up its tea. It thinks about hospital records. It had never found out what had happened to Thomas Echo; there had been no time between the incident and Rush's abduction. But now, the dream has made Dragon uneasy. It goes to the computer and hacks its way into the files of Our Lady of Mercy, the hospital closest to Lion Productions and the apartment of Thomas Echo.

With Dragon's computer experience and its agency training, scrambling the transmission and bypassing the hospital's weak security systems to access the medical files is not difficult. It scans through admissions and finds its lover's name on file, blinking hazily in golden script on the dark green screen.

It touches the screen to open Thomas Echo's file, and then it reads.

Dragon feels as if it has been physically struck in the chest with a baseball bat. All its breath leaves it in a slow, long rattle and then it gasps the air back in. Its body shaking, Dragon throws the tea cup against the computer screen which clatters then falls to the floor, the liquid spattering. Next, it picks up a chair and throws it full force. The screen shatters, red warning lights flickering on the console.

Woken by Dragon's sudden spike of distress, Blake runs into the room, eyes darting, body tense. "What happened?"

Dragon looks at its cousin. "He's dead," Dragon sputters. "I killed Thomas."

Blake stares, uncomprehending. Blake does not know who Thomas is. "So, what's the problem?" it asks.

Dragon feels its bile choking in its throat. Blake is not giving it any sympathy. Blake isn't doing anything. Blake is just standing there, unblinking, as casual as if Dragon had announced that it had lost a sweater and not the man it loves, so… so…

… so unfeeling.

Dragon launches the chair at Blake in a rage. Blake

was not expecting a projectile, but automatically ducks out of its path.

"Get out!" Dragon screams. "Get out of here, leave me alone!"

Blake, wordless, confusion clouding its face, backs out of the canteen, and Dragon is left alone with the anguish of its shattered heart in the shattered room.

♂

After a week of confinement in the brig by the ship's captain as punishment for destruction of property, Dragon returns. Stepping into its living quarters with a Thermos of fresh coffee in hand, it sees two Shamans sitting at the table. For a moment, the Shaper is startled, but then it realizes that one of them is just Blake assuming a different shape.

"Did you enjoy your time being locked up with Rush?" Blake asks.

Dragon stares enviously at Blake's wings, comparing them with the real thing. "Can you fly?" it asks, ignoring Blake's question.

Blake shrugs. "Ka'rael says it's something you learn when you're young. Might be a bit dangerous if I tried."

Dragon joins them at the table. "About Rush..." it says, pouring a cup of coffee for Blake and one for itself. "We have to find him something else to wear. He's starting to show."

Blake shrugs. Rush is not one of Blake's favorite topics. It toys with the coffee cup in front of it, thinking about what it's not going to say.

Dragon watches Blake thinking. It knows what Blake is thinking, but it decides to say what it wants to say anyway. "And I think it's time we let Rush out of his cell."

Blake rolls its eyes in a most dramatic manner. "Don't you – don't even – oh, forget it." Blake rises from the table with a heavy sigh. "Do what you want, Dragon Cello, you always do."

Dragon stares at its cousin as it walks away. "Blake, where're you going?"

"To take care of Rush."

"Shaped like that?"

Blake shrugs again, the feathers quivering with the movement of its shoulders, and then it leaves.

Dragon wraps its long fingers around the coffee cup and looks at Ka'rael. Beautiful, silent Shaman. "What did I say?"

The Shaman regards the Shaper with silent sympathy. Dragon stares back, sipping its coffee, waiting for a response. None comes.

"Well," Dragon says at last, "do you know what is wrong with Blake?"

"Well," the Shaman says, "do you really care?"

"Of course I care," Dragon says. "That's why I'm asking."

The Shaman gives it a long, scrutinizing look as though it were trying to decipher a hieroglyph on a pyramid wall. "Has it occurred to you that you've been acting selfish?"

The Shaper blinks in surprise. "Everyone's selfish."

"I'm not," Ka'rael says.

"Yes, but you're a different race altogether. It's not your nature."

"But is it in the Shapers' nature?"

"Oh," Dragon says slowly. "We do have a strong instinct for self-preservation."

"I believe that you've gone beyond self-preservation."

Dragon finds this negative criticism annoying. "What the fuck is that supposed to mean?"

Ka'rael pauses, sensing the Shaper's sensitivity, the raw wound still throbbing, hidden within. It knows that Dragon is indeed different from all the other Shapers that it has encountered (all two of them), and that Dragon has a tendency to react in a more emotional way. In fact, to react with any genuine emotion at all.

"Have you ever stopped to consider the consequences of your actions? Have you considered Blake? Or that maybe Blake doesn't want to go back to your homeworld?" the Shaman asks.

"Blake agreed to come," Dragon points out.

"Blake saw no other option to escape from the agency than the one that you presented, but that doesn't mean that Blake is happy about leaving Earth."

Dragon twists the cup, tracing concentric circles across the table, thoughtful. "I'm sorry that Blake isn't satisfied with how things turned out. But if we had stayed, they would have come after us. You know what they're like. They came after you."

"You came after me."

"I almost killed you."

"But you didn't."

"Maybe the next one would have."

"Maybe. But I managed to survive this long in the human world without any help."

Dragon pauses again, studying the Shaman's face, although its eye tends to always stray to those wings when they are unbound, as they are now, again wondering what it felt like to fly. "Are you saying that you didn't want to leave either?"

"I just want to be with you."

Dragon tries to picture Ka'rael at its side, living among the tribe. Although the tribe would allow it, the Shaman would always be an outsider. "What about your homeworld?"

The Shaman averts its eyes. "I can never return there."

"Why not? What happened to you?"

"It's a long story," the Shaman says quietly.

"I'd like it if you told me."

"I don't tell anyone this story," the Shaman whispers, pale with shame. "I never have."

"I would listen," Dragon says. "I want to understand you. I want to *know.*"

The Shaman sits in the silence that follows, thinking. It thinks about how it loves and trusts the Shaper, and how the Shaper sees the Shaman, actually sees and wants to understand it, and may even be beginning to love it. What is between them is strange, but it is beautiful, and that is important to Ka'rael.

"If you really want to know…" the Shaman trails off.

"Yes."

Ka'rael meets the Shaper's eyes again. "It would be easier if I showed you."

♂
♀

The sensation of falling into someone's internal landscape is indescribably strange and frightening, Dragon realizes, as it tumbles down into the Shaman's mind. The Shaper, despite the Shaman's implicit instructions, is losing control of itself, as though its identity were being torn into a hundred pieces. Drifting, it tries to hold onto a thread of its identity, repeating its own name to itself.

Dragon Cello, Dragon Cello, it says, but that bears little relevance to the actual identity of the Shaper, being not its true name but only one of a grand potential of personas the Shaper possesses. Thus the Shaper loses its grip on the thread that keeps its identity intact.

It floats, truly anonymous, blank-minded, through the Shaman's memories.

Eventually it lands, a field of flowers that resemble red poppies cushioning its fall. The Shaper uprights itself and scans its surroundings. All around it is a garden of Eden: lush green vegetation, rolling hills, clusters of fragrant blossoms, a myriad of colors. It spies a small, winged creature bathing in a clear, blue stream and approaches it.

As the Shaper approaches, the creature steps from the water onto the embankment, water sliding from its silver-sheened wings, dripping from its golden hair. It stares at the Shaper with large, mystical green eyes, the eyes of a child. Even as a child, the Shaman is hauntingly beautiful. It speaks to the Shaper in a language that it understands, but which language is unknown.

It says with a grave tone of voice, "They're coming, you know."

The Shaper does not know who "they" are, just as it does not know who it is or where it is or that this is actually a memory that lives inside the Shaman, one that has been permanently branded in its mind, one that has affected the Shaman all its life. Dragon has also forgotten all of the Shaman's warnings about how the Shaper was allowed to only observe the cycle of memory and should not, under any circumstance, become involved or upset the events which would occur. Senseless, the Shaper reaches out to place a hand on the beautiful face of the creature before it.

And then the Shaper melts into the Shaman. The Shaper disappears without a trace. The Shaper becomes.

♂

Blake checks the clip before snapping it back in the gun. The Glock is sleek and clean, well-oiled; Blake has been trained well in the use and maintenance of firearms. Clicking on the safety, Blake then places the gun in its pocket, picks up a pile of used clothes, and heads to the brig where Rush is.

Blake has decided that Rush is a threat to all of them.

Generally speaking, it is not in the Shapers' nature to murder, particularly a member of its own race. But Blake has, first of all, been considering the possible consequences if Dragon frees Rush like it wants to. Blake believes that Dragon is mentally sick because Blake senses something in its cousin that is not normal, something that Blake does not understand. Dragon's human act was no longer pretend, as far as Blake could tell, it was real. Second, Blake has not forgotten how Rush ordered the implanting of the anesthetic device around its Shaper mark nor the pain that was so excruciating that Blake almost died on the operating table, and hung between life and death for several days due to shock.

Blake never told Dragon about this experiment; it let Dragon think that it was due to some kindness on Rush's part that Dragon was not conscious for its own operation. Instead, the truth was that Rush could not afford the risk of losing Dragon to a simple surgical trauma. And, last of all, though paramount to Blake's decision, Blake didn't think that Rush was a *real* Shaper, that Rush had been permanently warped by the agency, so that he was an abomination to their race and therefore not to be trusted, and better off dead.

But the unborn child? Yes, Blake feels a twinge of regret for the loss of the child but, with Rush as its motherfather, it is possible that the blood of the child has been tainted. These things happened occasionally on the Shapers' homeworld, and those born with deformities were taken care of quickly, usually abandoned to die. Only one race, humans, allowed the sick and weak to survive. *Besides,* Blake reasons, *Dragon is young; it has the opportunity to bear three or four more children in its lifetime.*

Blake slips up to the cell where Rush is curled up in the corner sleeping, his arms wrapped around the swell of his belly which pushes out the bottom of his shirt and over the fastenings of his slacks. Blake sets the clothes down by the bars, then straightens up slowly. It watches Rush, defenseless in sleep, as it slides its hand into its pocket.

Rush's body twitches; he is dreaming. It is another Shaper dream. As the child grows in his womb, and as the ship sails closer and closer to the homeworld he has never seen, the Shaper dreams have been increasing in frequency and intensity. Now Rush wanders through the subconscious landscape, wearing his original shape.

In this dream, he is running through a dark wood, being chased. He trips, falls, and lands in Tamarac's arms. Although Rush has no solid memory of his motherfather, in the dream he recognizes the Shaper who now strokes his head in a maternal, protective fashion. But then the sense of safety is shattered as the men who were pursuing him emerge from the woods with their dully gleaming guns and machetes.

Rush howls in protest as a hail of bullets rips through Tamarac's body, spraying arcs of blood as it falls to the ground. Rush reaches for the corpse but then gloved hands are upon him, tearing him away. He screams, words flooding forth from his raw throat, his parched lips.

Blake withdraws the gun from its pocket, aiming it at the head of the sleeping Shaper and clicks off the safety as silently as possible.

It sees Rush's body jerk, and then Rush is mumbling, talking in his sleep. Blake is half-listening to the last words that Rush will ever say, and it recognizes some of the more coherent words.

"Motherfather... not me.. don't hurt... no... stop!" Rush mumbles.

Blake squeezes the trigger, slowly, smoothly, arm steady, eye on target, feels the inner mechanisms in the weapon start to move, but then Blake suddenly becomes aware of something that it should have noticed before, and it stops squeezing the trigger. Blake leans closer to the bars, listening to Rush, just to make sure that it has heard him properly.

Blake has suddenly become aware that Rush is not speaking English, although Blake understood portions of the one-sided dialogue of the dreamer. Blake understood because Rush is speaking the language he had never managed to learn in the confines of the agency: the oral language spoken by Shapers.

⚥

It hears its own name inside its mind, recognizes the sender as its parent. The familiar call fills the Shaman/Shaper with warmth for a moment, but then its body turns rapidly to ice. An overwhelming dread pins the Shaman/Shaper to the bank of the stream because it knows what is going to happen to it. It thinks to flee, but knows that escape is impossible. Resigning itself to its fate, it does not fly but walks home, each step heavy and slow, steeped in fear.

The Shaman/Shaper reaches home, and gives its customary embrace to its parents. It senses the love pouring out from one parent, and senses nothing from the other. It has been this way for as long as the Shaman/Shaper can remember. They say that its parent was damaged long ago, before the Shaman/Shaper's birth even, but no one has ever explained how it came to be. The Shaman/Shaper has heard the other children whispering in their minds about it, calling it "the child of the damaged one." In its language, this translates into "Ka'rael'anon." Teasingly, the others have given it the nickname of "Ka'rael," or "damaged one."

Ka'rael has come to believe this. It is aware that it is different from the other children its age. When its peers grew taller and became more lithe of form, Ka'rael barely added an inch. As its peers circled the sky with their bigger, more powerful wings, Ka'rael was left behind, unable to match pace with them. And, of course, there were its eyes. They were not the clear blue eyes of a Shaman, they were a mutated green. An ugly, ugly green. Ugly like Ka'rael is, compared to the others of its kind. Its body small and clumsy, his face too thin, his hair too dark, its wings underdeveloped and dull in color, the feathers frail. Ka'rael had heard other, crueler whispers that passed from mind to mind: that child, if it could have been foreseen at birth, would have been left on the rocks to feed the wild animals like the other crippled ones.

The door opens and two Shamans step in. No words are spoken. The Shaman/Shaper, although young, is perceptive enough to know why they have come. Silent and blindingly beautiful, the Shamans stand there in all their shimmering perfection. A moment passes before Ka'rael's parents become aware of their intentions. The undamaged parent falls to the floor, weeping perfect, golden tears. The others gesture for Ka'rael to accompany them. It has no other choice but to follow.

The Shaman/Shaper is brought to a rocky terrain on the outskirts of town. There are four other Shamans waiting for their arrival, each of them holding a stone casually in their hands, four perfect Davids waiting for the Goliath. The two Shamans which had led Ka'rael here also select a rock from the ground and then they all form a circle around the child. They lift their arms, golden fists punching the sky.

The Shaman/Shaper refuses to cry out as it is pelted with stones. A strike to the back of the knee causes it to fall to the ground. Its head is ringing with the pain as rocks rain down upon it. Finally it does cry out, its vision swimming as blood trickles into its eyes. It curls up into a fetal position, trying to protect itself with its arms and wings, but the brutal stoning continues, and it senses that it is dying as everything in its wavering vision turns the color of blood, like the time that Rush shot it with the Disabler ray in the parking lot of Lion Productions.

No, wait, thinks half of the child, *that was* me *in the parking lot of Lion Productions, and* this *me is* not me, *this never happened to* me. Then a word bursts out from the child, a word that resembles a coyote howl, jolted from its dormancy during its eight years on Earth. The true name of the Shaper shakes all of the Shaman's internal landscape and the Shaper is expelled from the child's body as though forced out by a giant gust of air. The Shaper shoots into the darkness and is falling once more.

⚥

Dragon scrambles out of the Shaman's naked limbs, gasping for air as though it had been drowning, and emits a strangled cry halfway between a yip and a bark.

Ka'rael's eyelids flutter open, and it stares at the

Shaper trembling beside it, and knows immediately that something is wrong. "Dragon...?"

Dragon places its head in its hands, violently twisting hunks of its own hair. "I'll kill them," the Shaper growls. "All of them must die!"

Ka'rael sits up, struggling against the crazy waves of rage and pain pouring from the Shaper, battering against Ka'rael's brain like that night in which Dragon had taken the Hammer. "Calm down, it will be all right," the Shaman says quickly in a soothing tone. "It's stressful to astral travel, even for my people. You need to sleep." It places a gentle hand on the Shaper's shoulder.

The Shaper, exhausted, its mind spinning, overreacts to the touch with more force than necessary. Meaning to push the Shaman's hand away, instead Dragon lashes out, striking the Shaman's face with a stinging slap. The Shaman is shocked for a moment, and then it starts to cry.

Dragon stares at it. Its eyes widen as it recognizes the creature in front of it. And yet the turbulent whirlpool of rage churns inside it, threatening to suck Dragon under completely. "Your people!" shouts the Shaper. "Your people – your own tribe – tried to murder you in cold blood because you... you..."

"Because I'm ugly," Ka'rael sobs.

Dragon can still feel the stones pelting its body, bruising flesh and breaking bone. "I don't understand you. I don't understand your people. They make me sick."

Ka'rael sobs harder. "Why are you doing this to me?" it wails. "I love you. I let you *inside* me..."

"You love me!" Dragon growls. Rage curls its large male hands into fists of stone. "What you love is this goddamn shape. It's beautiful, right? That's what your kind likes, isn't it? Only what's beautiful. Ka'rael. Damaged one."

Ka'rael wipes angrily at its tears. "Fuck you, Dragon."

Dragon laughs, cold and hollow. "You would if you could, angel child." It looks at the angry Shaman huddled unresponsive in the bed. "Tell me something."

"What?" says the Shaman reluctantly.

"How can you say you love me but not Blake or some other Shaper? Why *me?*"

"You're different. You're not like Blake. Blake has no feelings. Or Rush. Rush is..."

"Rush is what?" Dragon asks, suddenly defensive.

"Rush is... damaged."

Anger sizzles, a spark that slaps Ka'rael like a whip crack as Dragon becomes unhinged. "Don't talk about him that way!"

A pulse of fear jags Ka'rael's heart as Dragon leans closer, the skin around its eye not just twitching, but vibrating, pulsating with rage. "Don't... don't you touch me," Ka'rael whispers. "Dragon... please stop this... you're frightening me..."

Dragon seizes the Shaman on the bed and there is a struggle, a blur of arms, wings pummeling Dragon in the face. A wave of the Shaper's thoughts smash into the Shaman, a litany of *hurt hurt hurt.* Dragon reaches out, grasping one wing so tightly that the Shaman cries out in pain. The Shaper's other hand coils in the Shaman's hair, dragging the Shaman down below it, drawing the Shaman's face to its own.

"Do you know how many people I've killed?" Dragon shouts. "Do you know how easy it is? Do you know how easily I could have killed you?"

Fresh tears blur the Shaman's vision. "Then kill me!" it screams. "I can't live like this! I can't love an assassin!"

Something shifts in the Shaper's expression as it slides its hands around the Shaman's slender throat and then tightens its grip. The Shaman doesn't want to die; it gasps and tries to break free, clawing at the hands around its throat. Inside its flesh, Ka'rael's consciousness is trapped, crushed and withering below the overwhelming barrage of the Shaper's hatred and the *hurt hurt hurt.*

Let go of me! it tries to shout, but only a whispery gurgle emerges from its lips.

Then there is a sharp noise that Dragon immediately

recognizes as a gun shot. It turns its head toward the origin of the sound and sees Blake, who has been standing quietly in the threshold of the room for quite some time, gun in hand, still pointed in Dragon's direction. Dragon then looks at the wall by the bed and sees the hole where the bullet entered. Finally Dragon looks down at its torso and sees the hole where the bullet exited its body, a steady stream of blood already soaking into the sheets. The Shaper loosens its grip on the Shaman, who rapidly sucks in the air of which it has been deprived.

Dragon glances back at its cousin with sudden clarity. "Blake, you shot me."

Blake lowers the gun. "Yes, I did," it says calmly. "Don't make me do it again."

Dragon nods at Blake. "Right," it says, and then it faints.

♂

In the darkness, Dragon hears faint voices and the sound of someone softly weeping somewhere in the background. "Do you think a sedative might help?" someone asks. It is a woman's voice, unfamiliar. There is no answer. "Has the bleeding stopped?" asks the woman. "More or less," someone else says. It sounds like Blake.

Dragon opens its eyes and the blinding light above causes it to close its eyes again. It hears plastic rattling, switches clicking, and a steady pulse of electronic blips.

"Oh, that's no good," says the woman.

Blake rolls its eyes. "I think you need to work on your bedside manner, Doc."

"You mean lie to the patients," amends the ship's doctor. "Hate to say this, but I've never been good with that compassion thing."

"Well, then. You picked a fine career."

"At least it's a more noble profession to take bullets out of people than to put them in."

Blake smiles. "That depends on who you shoot."

"Hmm," says the doctor, looking at the X-ray. "You might have a point. But I see that the bullet has already made its exit. Clean, too. So, was there any particular reason that this Shaper was shot?"

"I felt sorry for Ka'rael. Dragon was strangling it," Blake says thoughtfully. "Actually, I've been kind of concerned about Dragon lately. He's been acting strangely. Out of control."

"Ka'rael – that's our unhappy camper?"

"Yes."

"Ka'rael," says the doctor. "You're going to damage your tear ducts if you continue on in that manner."

Ka'rael moans.

Dragon manages to open its heavy lids again, sees Blake standing above it, pressing cotton against the bullet wound in its abdomen. Dragon blinks for a moment, imagining that it's dreaming because Blake is still wearing the shape of a Shaman, wings unbound, and Dragon thinks that it's seeing the angel of death awaiting it. *It's better not to look*, Dragon decides, and promptly closes its eyes.

The doctor turns back to the X-ray. "You've made a bit of a mess in here."

"I didn't mean to. I was aiming for his ass. What's the problem? Can't it be fixed?"

The doctor adjusts her glasses, tucking a strand of black hair behind an ear. "There's not much I can do. There's been some damage here," she says, tapping the X-ray, where the bullet ripped through a knot-like clump of fibers which glow a pale orange-yellow on the monitor, "in the eighth major nerve bundle. I'm not equipped to do nerve repair. It's tricky business."

"Nerve damage?"

"Brain damage," the doctor says. "Maybe it's not too serious. Too soon to tell. And it's kind of strange."

"What do you mean, 'strange'?"

"The damage was sustained on the periphery of the nerve bundle, on what looks like a growth. I've never seen anything like it and I've no idea what it was doing there. The rest of the organ is intact so I don't foresee any problems with shifting."

"Oh," says Blake. It pauses a moment before asking, "How do you know so much about Shapers, anyway?"

The doctor laughs. "You mean you didn't sense it?" she asks. "I'm one of you."

♂

Dragon sleeps, a dreamless sleep.

Blake sleeps, dreaming of Lorenzo. In this dream, Blake is wearing a woman shape and Lorenzo is kissing Blake, but Blake finds his kisses boring and tells him so and then he starts to cry.

Rush sleeps, dreaming his homeworld tribal dreams.

The Shaper doctor sleeps, dreaming of its life on Earth, of its parent who had birthed it on the foreign planet nearly thirty years ago. It dreams of its childhood, playing with its younger brothersister on a well-kept green lawn in a small suburb outside of Chicago.

Ka'rael does not sleep. It remains at Dragon's bedside, keeping vigil over the Shaper's healing body, surrounding the Shaper with all its love and devotion.

The ship continues to move towards the Shaper's homeworld.

Rush wakes up, screaming in pain.

The doctor wakes up, sensing Rush's pain, without recognizing the source.

Blake wakes up, sensing Rush's pain, recognizing that it's Rush.

Dragon sleeps, the sleep of someone who has traveled a great distance through someone's internal landscape and can do nothing but sleep, and will not wake up until it is time.

Ka'rael, too, senses Rush's pain, but will not leave Dragon's side.

The doctor stumbles into the ward in its pajamas

and surveys the scene, seeing that everything is calm. Then the doctor mumbles to itself and goes to the Shapers' room, knocking on the door.

"Come in," calls Blake.

The doctor steps in, recognizes Blake who is now wearing one of its female human shapes, as it was too difficult to sleep with the wings it had formed, sitting up in bed.

"Are you all right?" the doctor asks.

"Just peachy," says Blake.

"Then, Jesus, I must have been dreaming or something. I could've sworn that there was a Shaper in pain."

"You weren't dreaming."

"But it wasn't Dragon and it wasn't you… I don't get it."

Blake runs a hand through its pale hair. "Oh, you wouldn't know, would you? There's another Shaper on board. It's Rush. I felt it, too. Woke me up, that bastard."

"Where is it?"

"Incarcerated."

"What for?"

"Long story," says Blake. "I doubt you'd even believe me. It would probably make a good movie, though. A real thriller."

"You can tell me about it later," says the doctor. "Let's go."

Blake sighs. "Do I have to?"

"Yes, come on, get up."

Blake sighs again and throws back the bedsheets.

The Shapers move through the dark, quiet corridors which are programmed to emulate the sensation of night against the infinite darkness of the space beyond. "Is this Rush dangerous?"

"I'd say so. He used to kill and torture people for a living."

"A Shaper? What for?"

Blake shrugs. "Secret Service shit."

"Ah. I've heard rumors."

"Rumors don't usually amount to anything," Blake says, "but in this particular case, I'm sure that the truth is even worse than the rumor."

They arrive at Rush's cell. Rush is huddled in one corner, his head hanging down, knees drawn up. His body is shaking.

"Rush?" calls the doctor.

Rush lifts his head and regards them with eyes that are black from pupil to edge, his skin no longer a cream color, reverting back to its natural brown. "I... I... can't hold the shape."

A shiver courses up the doctor's spine to see a Shaper in such a state. "Something's wrong."

The Rush shape completely shifts away and then only a dark-skinned Shaper like any other remains. "Help... me..." Rush says, faltering in its native tongue. "Want... Dragon." It stretches out its legs, revealing the flushed skin stretched over its swollen belly, which is rippling with movement from within.

"Oh, shit," the doctor says. "Blake, I think you'd better find someone to unlock this cell so I can deliver this baby."

☿

Dragon wakes and sees Ka'rael at its bedside, green eyes red from tears and exhaustion. Its eyes are lakes of sorrow. "Dragon, are you okay?"

Dragon stares at the Shaman. "I suppose so," it says finally. "And you?"

"I've been better."

Dragon sits up carefully. "What are you doing here?"

"I was worried about you."

Dragon looks away from the Shaman. "But I tried to kill you. Don't you hate me?"

"Well, no," Ka'rael admits. "I mean, I did hate you at first," it says, and Dragon returns its gaze to the Shaman's face. "But then I... I..." the Shaman trails off, disturbed by the blank, unblinking expression on the Shaper's face. The

Shaman tries to swallow, but its throat has become suddenly tight. "Dragon?"

Dragon is thinking about how the Shaman loves it. It is thinking about Thomas Echo, about what it felt. It remembers very clearly what it felt, the love, the desperation, the fear, and the anger, but there is something strange about the memory, as though it had been a movie that Dragon had seen and not what it had actually experienced. "What?"

Ka'rael's blood has turned to ice in its veins. It senses nothing from the Shaper before it. "Dragon... how do you feel? I mean, what are you feeling right now?"

Dragon considers this. It searches inside itself for something to give. Dragon does not feel bad, actually, all of its anger has fled, all the dark, tangled confusion, the guilt, the shame and the angst; all faded into nothing more than a memory. The Shaper feels normal, that is, normal for one of its kind. It looks at the desperate creature before it, not necessarily wanting to hurt it, but seeing no reason to lie.

"I feel... nothing," it says.

PART 6.
NARCISSUS IS DREAMING

Seven years pass.

♂

The figure stands at the edge of the shadow, the comfortable darkness blurring the lines between background and body, shadows caressing the folds of its black clothing so that nearly no distinction can be made between animate and inanimate in the empty warehouse. It remains extremely still, its gray eyes unblinking – eyes as cold and hard as steel – as it surveys the damp street below, waiting. Only the eyes are in motion, flickering back and forth from one end of the street to the other, and one slim, pale hand which steadily brings a burning cigarette to its lips every thirty seconds or so, and then dips into the dark again, a cherry-red spark hissing like a warning signal against its thigh.

A noise rattles up from the street below: a vagrant knocking over a garbage can. The figure watches, unblinking, until the vagrant wanders off. Then it drops the cigarette and reaches for a netbook that has been resting on a chair to its right. On the screen is the image of a young man with crazy, snake-like hair twisting out in all directions. A boy that looks like someone who was once called Thomas Echo. In reality, the boy in the picture is a nineteen-year-old actor named Faust Rossellini.

But this is not reality. This is only a film.

Max Pride stands at the back of the theater. But he's not looking at the screen. He's looking at the audience which is full of Tiradians and a handful of human tourists. He suspects that the audience is actually a crowd of Shapers, dressed up in inconspicuous shapes for the film premiere the way some people dress up in finery to attend opening night at the opera. He is looking for someone but recognizes no one.

The film, which was banned on Earth because the writer, Kincaid O'Bryan, insisted on calling it a "docu-drama," continues to roll over the screen. The title of the film is *Narcissus is Dreaming*. Critics all over the planet had a blood fest with the censors who'd dared to stifle the work of such a renowned and talented artist such as Kincaid O'Bryan, whose latest works had firmly established him as one of the greatest contemporary writers in the universe, but the censors won. So Lion Productions took the film off-world. Now, a few months later, Max Pride is anticipating a great success at the premiere in the City of the Cascades.

Max watches the audience closely, hopeful that someone will meet his eye, will show some sign of recognition, but hardly anyone gives him a glance. All eyes are riveted to the screen.

On the screen, the story unfolds. Two men in dark suits who say that they are off-world promoters come to talk to the writer and the director of the film inside the film. In the next scene, a young girl meets a beautiful man in a bar, then they are at her house.

What's your name, anyway? she says.

Dragon, he says.

Dragon what?

Dragon Cello.

Towards the end of the film, Kincaid steps into the theater and stands beside Pride. "Well?" he whispers.

"She's not here."

"You mean 'it,'" Kincaid corrects. "Are you sure?"

"Hell, no," Pride admits. "For all I know, our 'Dahlia' could be dead by now, or gone from this planet." He shrugs. "I thought you weren't coming tonight."

Kincaid makes a vague gesture. "I wasn't going to, but I changed my mind at the last minute."

"You were sleeping when I left the hotel."

"Woke up. Decided to come down and see how you were doing, so… well, how're you doing?"

"Strangely disappointed."

"But the theater is packed with people."

"Yeah, well, I was looking for a particular person and she – it – is not here."

"But you can't be sure of that, you said so yourself," Kincaid points out.

Pride shrugs again. "One of life's little ironies for you. You can know a shit load about Shapers and still not recognize one, even if it's staring you right in the fucking face."

The audience applauds enthusiastically as the credits roll over the screen, and the people start to drain out of the theater. Pride and Kincaid wait to see if anyone lingers or attempts to talk to them, but, in the end, they are the only ones left.

"Ah, fuck it," says Pride. "Let's go."

On the street, Kincaid passes Pride a cigarette and the men light up. The air is warm, the sky dotted with bright stars, and flowers from the banks of the Cascades are releasing fragrant pollen into the city.

"Beautiful night," Kincaid remarks.

"*Hai*," Pride agrees, smoking silently for a moment, feeling the night around them. "*Ne*, let's go see how Ophelia and Mell are doing."

Kincaid glances down the street, in the opposite direction of the hotel. "You know, I think I'm going to take a walk. I'll see you later, Max, okay?"

"Sure," Pride says, and then grins. "Don't do anything that I wouldn't do."

"Oh, I probably will," Kincaid says and laughs, as they head off in opposite directions. A few steps away, Kincaid stops and turns. "*Ne*… Max?"

Pride turns, sees Kincaid's blond hair and cigarette

standing out against the dark. "What?"

Kincaid takes a long final drag off his cigarette before he says, "Eh. Never mind. I'll tell you later," he says, then turns and continues down the street, until his body disappears, swallowed by the dark.

Pride shakes his head, murmuring to himself, then turns and heads back towards the hotel. Yes, he is rather disappointed that he didn't get to see the Shaper. Every now and then he wonders how the story ended: what happened to Rush, to Blake, to the child. He knew that the ship carrying the fugitive Shapers had docked on Tiradia as scheduled seven years ago, but that was all he knew. An unfinished story. A film without an end.

He enters the hotel room and finds Ophelia sitting on the couch with a netbook in her lap, music playing softly in the background. A four year old girl runs up and squeezes Pride's legs.

"Daddy, you're home!"

"Mell, don't shout," Ophelia says. Pride scoops up his daughter and kisses her, then leans over to kiss his wife. "How was the premiere?" she asks.

"A smashing success, of course," says Pride. "After all, the whole universe is aware of how truly great I am."

"Yeah, yeah," says Ophelia.

"Yeah, yeah," mimics Mell.

"Yeah, yeah," comes a voice from the adjoining bedroom.

Max freezes in his tracks. He knows that voice well. He sets Mell down in Ophelia's arms and goes to the bedroom. Sprawled half-naked in a tangle of sheets is Kincaid O'Bryan.

"What the fuck are you doing here?" Pride snaps.

"What the fuck does it look like I'm doing?" he retorts with a sleep-encrusted voice. "I'm fucking sleeping."

"Have you been here the whole time?"

"*Hai.*"

"Ophelia, has Kincaid been here the whole time?"

"Yes, dear."
"Oh, Christ," Pride grumbles.
"*Nanda?*" Kincaid asks. "What is it?"
"Fucking hell!" Pride roars.
"What? What? What happened?"
"One of life's little ironies," says Pride.

ACKNOWLEDGMENTS

First and foremost, I'd like to thank Adam Bogle, for Lion Productions was entirely his idea, and where the story started. I'd also like to thank his wife, Sophia Wolohan Bogle, who was the first person to read and critique *Narcissus is Dreaming*, and who wisely showed me where the story needed to end.

I would also like to thank my editor, Stacy Giufre, for believing in this book, for all her hard work and support, and for the best comment I've ever received from an editor: "Make it more 'I love you. But fuck you.'" I surely owe you more than one cocktail at the Abbey.

One word of writing advice often trotted out is to never put real people you know into your fiction. This is advice I have completely ignored, as *Narcissus* is populated with characters I have known in real life. Therefore, I would also like to acknowledge the following people who have, in one way or another, inspired this work: Allon Beausoleil, Amy Cook, Nik Edgerton, Daniel Ferry, JC Karrantza, Akhrijatun, Jeremy, Jordan Tao, Kamela, Keenan, Sergio and, of course, Jason Rush, whose name was just too perfect to change, despite not actually deserving to be the bad guy, at least for the reason of being the only man to write me a story about the sun.

Finally, I would like to thank my parents and all the Pink Narc minions for putting up with my shit all these years. You are all worth more than salt.

ABOUT THE AUTHOR

Michael D. Takeda is a writer of speculative fiction that has been called "dark" by *Publishers Weekly* and whose gender-bending themes *Analog* has compared to those of Theodore Sturgeon. He has also worked as a translator and teacher of English and Italian language and cinema, had a brief stint as a music reviewer for local newspaper "PDXS," completed two degrees in Italian literature, and has published various fictions. He currently lives in Worcester, Massachusetts where he attends nursing school and serves as Editor in Chief of Pink Narcissus Press.

Michael may know a thing or two about switching genders. His most recent project is *Brave Boy World: A Transman Anthology* (2017, Pink Narcissus Press). For more information, visit his website at elvesfromiceland.weebly.com.

Other science fiction titles available from
PINK NARCISSUS PRESS

THE BIRTHDAY PROBLEM

A science fiction novel by Caren Gussoff
"Gussoff packs a punch in this multi-layered and beautiful narrative. Strange and wonderful, *The Birthday Problem* presents a Pacific Northwest fractured and transformed, but always well worth the visit." – Cat Rambo, author of *Near + Far*
ISBN: 978-1-939056-06-1

DAUGHTERS OF ICARUS

New Feminist Science Fiction and Fantasy
"Throughout, the authors explore themes of gender, identity, and autonomy, with characters as diverse as miniature clones, stripper vampires, aggressive mermaids, and mystical crones. Many of the stories focus on gender roles and the pull of relationships, whether parental, familial, or romantic, among all kinds of people." —*Library Journal*
ISBN: 978-1-939056-00-9

BRAVE BOY WORLD

A Transman Anthology
"This is really an anthology about gender, both male and female, with some valuable insights into both branches of the transgender experience. Michael Takeda has really done a fantastic job of gathering such a deep, diverse collection." —*Bending the Bookshelf*
ISBN: 978-1-939056-12-2